GENETIC
REMEMBRANCE

ACKNOWLEDGEMENTS

I would like to express my deep appreciation to the following people: Ms. Nancy Hauser for her primary editing, Mr. Colin Borsos for proof-reading this novel, and finally Mr. James Norman for the final editing, typesetting and publication of this novel.

PREFACE

Ever since I was in my teens, ancient Buddhist and Daoist documents have always fascinated me. In many documents there is mention of how, when a meditator had developed a high level of subconscious mind, he or she would be able to communicate with the spiritual world through energy vibrations. This capability was called "Shen Tong" (spiritual communication) in Chinese Qigong society. It is said that once you have established the capability of synchronizing your spiritual energy vibration with Nature's, you will be able to access all memories or knowledge recorded in the past.

It was also mentioned in *The Book of Change* (*Yi Jing*) and the *Dao De Jing* that there are two dimensions or worlds coexisting in Nature: one is the material world, called Yang World (Yang Jian), while the other is the spiritual world, called Yin World (Yin Jian). Though there are two worlds in function, it is only one since both worlds synchronize with and influence each other simultaneously. The Yin World is called the Dao while the Yang World is called the De in the book, *Dao De Jing*. It is also stated that the Dao (Spiritual World) is the mother of the nature that produces everything and the De (Material World) is the manifestation of the Dao.

As we all know, though we have already acquired a good level of knowledge regarding the material sciences, we still have not learned much or gained much insight into the spiritual sciences. For example: How does our brain function? What is the Spirit? Is Mind some sort of power that when manifested can change the whole world? How is our mind related to spirit? Are we able to understand the spiritual world and access it through scientific developments? Is the spiritual world the same as that mostly unknown matter scientists call "dark matter" or "dark energy"? Will we be able to travel in the Yin World and reach other civilizations? All of these questions are still waiting to be answered.

In the past, due to a lack of understanding of spiritual science, religions were created to interpret the spirit. Unfortunately, these attempts have often been used as a tool to dominate and restrict humans' spiritual development. From these spiritual abuses and bondage, dogmas were created, and countless wars were, and still are, initiated. I believe that the last century was a material century, since during it we developed a high level of material enjoyment. It is very unfortunate that due to these successes, we have also created the possibility of human catastrophe. The question is, if 100 nuclear bombs are able to wipe out the entire human race, why do we need more than 7,000 bombs on this earth, ready to kill each other? Are we crazy? If the entire human race is not able to wake up and bring their awareness and alertness to a new level spiritually, I believe a tragic human future can be foreseen. I hope by the end of this century we are able to awaken and develop a high level of spiritual understanding. This is the solution for the future of humankind.

I intend to use this novel to inspire readers to think deeply, and hopefully encourage them to meditate and develop their subconscious feelings. This will provide us with a higher level of awareness and alertness. Without these two elements, we will be on the path of self-destruction.

Dr. Yang, Jwing-Ming
YMAA CA Retreat Center
Miranda, CA
December 20, 2018

GENETIC CONNECTION

It was a gloomy day in autumn, with low hanging clouds and a chill wind blowing. Marek Müller stood to the left of his mother. His sister was on his mom's right and two younger brothers were on his left. Two uncles, along with many other people, were on the other side of the grave. They were all watching a coffin being lowered slowly down into the ground. He could see that his mom and two uncles' faces were twisted in grimaces of deep sorrow. His sister was sobbing. As for himself, Marek felt emotionless, just numb and lost. In this detached state, he was not sure who was being buried. He thought the person must be someone very close to him. All he could think of, from his observation of the scene around him, was that this dead person was his father.

CHAPTER 1. PRESENT

This was the fourth time in the last two months that Marek was awakened by the same nightmare. The scene in the dream was so vivid. Marek could see everyone's face somewhat clearly and yet he could swear that he had never met any of them in his life, including those people his dream-self had thought of as his mother, brothers, sister, and uncles. He wondered where these dreams were coming from, as well as why, and how they came to be.

"I must be crazy!" he thought.

Marek always woke from these nightmares with a feeling of sadness and of being lost. He did not understand what the dreams meant or implied.

"Is this a hint that someone close to me is going to die?" he wondered. But then, "No, definitely not. Judging from the clothes and setting in the dream, it wasn't happening in the present day. It was a scene from the past, a long time ago. But who were those people I have never met?" His mind was confused. "Well! It was only a dream," he told himself.

Marek tossed around in bed for a while but could not fall asleep again. He looked over at his wife, Stephanie, lying next to him, still sound asleep. Finally, he got up quietly and tried not to wake her. It was only 3:30 in the morning.

Going into the living room Marek saw his wedding photo on the wall, along with a few others they had taken over the last months of his two sons, Erik, 7 years old, and Steffen, 5. He smiled.

The pictures reminded Marek of his wedding day 11 years ago in 1988. He had been 32 and his wife only 26. Now, he was already 43 and felt that he was the luckiest person in the whole world. He had a nice and supportive wife and two great boys. In addition, business at his company, Müller's Import & Export, Inc., was booming. The value of stock in his company, and in all of the stock market, kept going up and up; it seemed there was no end to it.

"1999 is a great year, indeed," Marek thought.

Marek went into his study where, in the corner, there was a meditation cushion and a pillow. Usually, he woke up around 5:30 in the morning and meditated for an hour. Stephanie would be up, as usual, at 6:30 and would prepare breakfast for the family. Marek settled onto the cushion and, after taking a few deep breaths, he felt his thoughts calm down as his body entered a state of deep relaxation. He began to search for the feeling in the center of his head, the limbic system, where the subconscious mind is located.

MEDITATION

Marek had begun practicing yoga meditation in 1992 and, since then, he had been meditating almost every morning. He was pretty lucky that his wife supported his meditation since she knew that the practice might help him release a lot of the stress he dealt with in his business.

Only a year ago, through his friend, Steve Zhang, Marek had learned about Chinese Embryonic Breathing Meditation. Steve had been his best pal in high school. He was an ABC (American Born Chinese) - both his parents were from Taiwan originally. Steve was always interested in Chinese culture, especially anything related to spiritual cultivation.

Later, when Marek went to Babson College in Wellesley, Massachusetts, Steve stayed in Chicago and majored in physics at Chicago State University. After graduating, Marek moved back to Chicago to stay with his mom. Both Marek and Steve were busy pursuing their careers, but they called each other regularly and got together occasionally.

Marek remembered a year ago, when a rare chance had brought Steve to East Chicago for a conference. Since he would be in the area, Steve had called Marek and invited him to meet for lunch. During lunch, they started chatting about meditation.

"I didn't know you have been meditating for six years. I also meditate and enjoy it very much. What kind of meditation are you doing?" Steve asked.

"Yoga meditation. I learned it from a yoga teacher on the east side of Chicago six years ago. I have been practicing it since then. It's helped me relax and eased my stress. I feel so peaceful and calm after meditation each time. What meditation are you practicing?" Marek asked.

"Actually, I practice Chinese Embryonic Breathing Meditation. I learned it three years ago from a retired Qigong Master in Northern California. The amazing thing is, through this kind of meditation I am not only relaxed and have a calm and peaceful mind, but I am also able to trace back to the beginning of my life as an embryo, and regain the feeling of being natural, soft, and naïve like an infant. Now, as I am getting deeper and deeper in my meditation, I begin to feel or sense nature and a connection with the spiritual world," Steve said.

"What do you mean "feel like an infant?" What is Embryonic Breathing Meditation? It sounds great but mysterious. And when you talk about the spiritual world, that just feels spooky," Marek laughed.

"Okay, Marek, be serious. Like I said, when you reach a high level in Embryonic Breathing Meditation, it can bring you back to the beginning of your life, like an embryo in your mother's womb. You feel simple, pure, and innocent. In that state, you are able to reattach to your natural spirit through a profound depth of feeling. When it happens, your sense of time and the material world disappear. What I mean is, this meditation helps you minimize your conscious mind's activities and wakes up your subconscious mind and feelings. You know, it is the subconscious mind in our limbic system that is more truthful and connected with nature," Steve explained.

"The most amazing part is once you minimize the activities of your conscious mind, anything disturbing you emotionally, or binding you so that you can't think clearly, will disappear. I mean you could set yourself free from the human matrix or from emotional bondage. It is called 'regulating the mind' in meditation. Remember, your mind is like a military general governing all of your body's functions, both mentally and physically. If your mind is chaotic and confused, your Qi circulation will become disordered," Steve continued.

"What is Qi? I have heard about Qi and Qigong, but don't really know what they are," Marek asked. His curiosity had become engaged and he was interested to know more.

"In Chinese culture, any type of energy existing in nature is called Qi. For example, weather is called 'Tian Qi,' meaning 'heaven Qi.' Air is called 'Kong Qi,' meaning 'space energy.' Air conditioning is called 'Leng Qi,' which means 'cold Qi,' and heat is called 'Re Qi,' which means 'hot Qi.' From these examples, you can see that there are all types of energy called 'Qi.' When Qi is applied to humans, it is called 'Ren Qi' and means 'human Qi.'"

"Interesting! That means Qi is everywhere in this universe, right?" Marek said.

"Bingo! You are smart, you know," Steve laughed. "As we have come to understand about the human body, when it is alive it includes both a physical aspect and an energy aspect. This energy aspect, or part, is human Qi. The Qi in the body is the foundation of life, and when the Qi's circulation becomes disordered, then we get sick or even die."

"Are you implying that Qi is the foundation of your health? It sounds like Prana in yoga."

"I believe so. When this Qi is applied to a human body, it is known as bioelectricity today. If you can understand this, then you will understand what Qigong is. Gong means 'Gongfu' in Chinese and means 'time and energy.' Anything that takes time and energy to accomplish is called 'Gongfu.' That means Qigong is 'the hard study or practice of Qi.' When this term is applied to the human body, Qigong means the study and practice of the body's function or activities related to Qi's storage, circulation, and manifestation."

"Wow! Amazing! How do you know so much?" Marek was very surprised that Steve knew so much. He had never talked about meditation with his friend before.

"Well! I am Chinese. And I grew up in a Chinese family influenced by Chinese culture. These concepts were very common in Chinese society. It is just yoga in an Indian mind."

Steve went on, "When Qigong is applied to and practiced by people, there are different levels and purposes. Medical Qigong is the search for ways to maintain Qi's smooth circulation in the body so sickness can be prevented or healed. Scholar Qigong is looking for ways meditation can bring the mind to a peaceful and calm state. Religious groups, such as Buddhists or Daoists, are aiming for spiritual enlightenment. Finally, for martial artists, Qigong is the training they do to increase their awareness, alertness, power, and endurance."

"Then how does Embryonic Breathing Meditation fit in with these Qigong practices?" Marek asked.

"In my opinion, Embryonic Breathing Meditation is the root or foundation of all Qigong practices. It talks about two poles in a human body that are related to our spiritual and physical lives. It also teaches you how to regulate or manage these two lives."

"Amazing! How long have the Chinese people been practicing Embryonic Breathing Meditation? It sounds so wonderful."

"Well! I believe that the very beginning of Embryonic Breathing Meditation was from Lao Zi's *Dao De Jing*. You know, the Chinese have been heavily influenced by three main writings that built up the foundation of Chinese culture. The first book is *Yi Jing, The Book of Change*; the second, *Dao De Jing*; and the third is Confucius' *Lun Yu, Analects*,"

Steve tried to explain.

"This is becoming too complicated for me now. Just tell me what you know about Embryonic Breathing Meditation. I am more interested in knowing how to do that, but we don't have much time left. We need to go back to work," Marek pointed out.

"Basically, there are a few goals that you want to reach in Embryonic Breathing practice. First, you want to regulate your mind until you have minimized your conscious mind's activities. That allows your subconscious mind to wake up and feel nature. Next, you want to use your subconscious mind to lead the Qi to your body's Qi center so it can be stored to an abundant level. The final goal is to unite your spirit and Qi at the Real Dan Tian. That is a term that refers to the physical center of your body, where your guts are. When this happens, you will feel the Qi gathered in this center as an embryo in its mother's womb," Steve said.

"Why would we want to do that, Steve? I mean, what is the purpose?"

"You know, there are two very important purposes in Qigong practice. One is to have a healthy and long life. The second is to cultivate your spirit to a higher level. To reach these two goals, you need to have an abundant storage of Qi because without enough energy you just can't do anything. In addition, you also need a high level of focus and a powerful mind or spirit so the Qi can be manifested efficiently. This is the quality of Qi's manifestation. Without these two basic criteria, you can't go anywhere. Embryonic Breathing Meditation provides you the theory and technique to have a powerful mind and also to store the Qi to an abundant level at your Lower Dan Tian. Again, I mean the center of your physical body, where the bio-battery is located.

"In order to have a high level of spirit, so the Qi can be manifested efficiently, you must minimize the function of your conscious mind. Instead you want to bring your subconscious mind to a higher level of awareness and alertness. When your subconscious mind is awakened and reaches to a high level, you will be able to reconnect with nature. As you know, due to the domination of the material world on our conscious minds throughout our human history, we have increasingly isolated ourselves from nature. This has been going on for too long already. We have created an entire human matrix, or dogma, that we are now trapped within," Steve continued.

"Why do we want to minimize our conscious mind? I thought being more conscious and aware would give you a higher level of concentration," Marek asked.

"The truth is that whenever the conscious mind generates a thought, it plays games. Conscious thinking often makes us become sneakier, more cunning, and untruthful. However, when you stop thinking and allow the feeling of your subconscious mind to direct your practice, you will be able to reconnect to your natural spirit. Doing things subconsciously is what Lao Zi called 'Wuwei,' or doing nothing. For example, if you set up a scheduled time for Qigong practice and do it then and only then, pretty soon you will quit due to laziness and impatience. However, if you build up a habit and practice Qigong without thinking, then you are doing it without doing it. The most powerful Qigong practice is to blend practice into your daily life so that it becomes routine or habit," Steve said.

"Now I am really curious and very interested. You have told me the What and the Why of Embryonic Breathing Meditation. So, can you tell me How you do it?" Marek's mind kept thinking about what Steve had told him.

"Well, first you have to find your mental center. I mean you must be able to feel your limbic system at the center of your head where your subconscious mind is. Once you can feel it, then through correct breathing, you lead your mind and Qi there. When the Qi is led away from the brain to this center, the conscious mind will be downplayed. Slowly, your subconscious mind will be set free. You know, it is our conscious mind, or the dogmas in our mind, that restricts our spiritual growth," Steve explained.

"Hey Steve, let me repeat what I just heard you say and see if I understand this correctly. The first step is leading your mind to the center of your head, the limbic system, so the Qi in the brain can also be led to this center. When this happens, the activities of your conscious mind will be minimized and the subconscious mind that is situated in the limbic system will be able to wake up, right?" Marek asked.

"Amazing. You are a genius. It took me a long while to figure out that whole concept," Steve praised.

"Wait! I still have two questions. First, once I can feel the limbic system, how do I lead the Qi there? Second, once the subconscious mind is awakened and reaches to a higher level, how do I reconnect to nature?" Marek asked.

"Now you are thinking deeply! The answer to your first question is 'inhalation longer then exhalation.' You know as we breathe, when our exhale is longer than our inhale our Qi extends outward. When our inhale is longer than our exhale, our Qi is condensed inward. For example, when you are excited and laugh, subconsciously you exhale longer than inhale. When this happens, you become hot and your heartbeat gets faster. When you are sad or scared, without thinking, you inhale longer than exhale. In this case, you begin to feel chilly and your heartbeat slows down. From this example you can see that the first trick is keeping your mind at the limbic system while inhaling longer than exhaling. This will allow the Qi to gather at the limbic system and bring your subconscious mind to a higher awakening state. When you have reached a good level, you will be in a semi-sleeping state."

"Then what's the next step?" Marek asked anxiously.

"Once you have stabilized your mental center, then you must find your energy center or Qi center, which is called the Real Lower Dan Tian in Qigong. Dan Tian means 'elixir field.' This area is able to grow 'elixir' or the Qi that is able to extend your life. Actually, this Qi center is also your physical center, located at the center of the line connecting the top of your two pelvic bones. It is the center of gravity in western science. This is the location of the bio-battery I mentioned earlier. This is also the place of women's wombs where they carry their babies. You know babies develop in this place because Qi is so important for growth."

"Now I wish I were a woman so I could feel my womb. Unfortunately, I am not," Marek said with a laugh. "Seriously, tell me how I can feel it and find it?"

"Actually, it's easier to find this physical center than the mental center. Just picture that a ring surrounds your waist. The center of the ring is where the Qi center is," Steve said.

"Once you find the center, so what? I mean, what's next?"

"Then you synchronize the mental center and the Qi center simultaneously. You know, these two centers must coordinate with each other smoothly and harmoniously," Steve continued.

"Then what?" Marek asked again as he looked at his watch. Suddenly, he realized that it was getting late. Both of them needed to get back to work.

"Then, you bring your mind down to the Qi center and stay there. This is the crucial key to Qi storage." Steve glanced down at his watch too, realizing that they didn't have time to continue. "Sorry, Marek. To know Embryonic Breathing Meditation to a profound level, you have to know more. But we are running out of time."

"Wow! You are so great! All of this is new to me. Where did you get all of this knowledge? Where can I get more information?" Marek asked with interest and enthusiasm.

"You can find books and videos with all of this information just doing a Google search on the internet. You know, you can find almost anything on the internet. We are in an era of knowledge explosion. As long as you are willing to learn, plenty of information is there for you.

"I'm sorry, but it's getting late and I need to go back to my conference. Ha, ha! You know, plug myself into the matrix again, otherwise I'll be fired. Not like you, since you are your own boss. After all, we all became money slaves once money was created, right? Adiós, my friend." Steve stood up, took his wallet out and got ready to pay.

"Steve, just go! This is my treat. I have learned so much from you just in one hour," Marek said with a big grin.

Since Marek owned his own company, he did not have to be as rushed to get back to work. He sat and pondered Steve's words for a while. He had always been interested in spiritual cultivation. It was because of this that he was so interested in hypnosis and meditation. He resolved to find more information on the relationship between Qigong and the *Dao De Jing*, as well as about the meditation theory and methods of Embryonic Breathing Steve had talked about.

Even after Marek had returned to his office, he was still excited about the conversation he had had with Steve. He took care of some important business first, then did a Google search for Embryonic Breathing Meditation. Much to his surprise, he found both books and DVDs on the topic. He ordered some online and received them just a week later. He also found a book called *Dao De Jing – Qigong Interpretation* on Amazon.com and ordered that as well. He began to read the books and watch the DVDs whenever he had time.

THE SIGN

After a whole year of study and practice, Marek had achieved a basic idea of how Embryonic Breathing Meditation worked and felt. As Steve had said, the first step was minimizing the action of his conscious mind and bringing his subconscious mind to a higher state of awareness and alertness. The crucial key to achieving this was using correct breathing methods to bring his mind and Qi to the limbic system of his head.

This morning, after only 20 minutes, Marek's mind had already been calmed and he had gradually entered a semi-sleeping stage; his conscious mind had given up its domination. He was in the state of 'thinking of no thinking,' pure and innocent. Slowly, he was able to re-attach to the nature that made him feel so simple, pure, and comfortable. It seemed all of his emotions - glory, dignity, happiness, joy, sadness - all disappeared. The mask on his face – the ways of acting and feeling he had developed to function in society - dropped off and he became his more truthful self. He was able to jump out of the human matrix mentally when he meditated. This brought him to a high level of relaxation and, most importantly, a calm and peaceful mind.

Suddenly, the scene from his dream appeared in his subconscious mind. He was so surprised to see it. However, once he paid attention to it, the feeling disappeared. This was the first time the funeral scene appeared in his meditation instead of in his sleep. He knew that once his conscious mind dominated his thinking, the subconscious feeling would be suppressed. He tried to bring his mind back to a state of subconscious self-hypnosis, or semi-sleeping, but failed. He knew that was the end of his meditation for now.

Getting up, he went to the kitchen to look for something to eat.

"Good morning, Marek. Sleep well?" Stephanie asked as she stepped into the kitchen.

"Good morning, Stephanie. I hope I didn't wake you up." Marek looked at her with a smile as he poured rice milk into a glass.

"No, you didn't. It's almost 7 o'clock already. Don't you have to get ready for work?"

"Yes, I do. It is Tuesday, you know. Oh, you better wake up Erik. His school bus will be here in 40 minutes," Marek said.

As usual, they let Steffen sleep late since he was only 5 years old. Stephanie would take him to kindergarten at 8:30 a.m. She went to wake Erik and, when she returned, Marek was standing near the sink with a thoughtful expression on his face.

"Stephanie, remember the funeral scene that I told you about? The one keeps appearing in my dreams. It appeared during my meditation this morning! I don't know what it is or why it keeps showing up! I just can't figure it out!" Marek exclaimed.

"Maybe you are just too stressed from work? Maybe something

has bothered you deep in your heart?" Stephanie smiled at him and pointed her finger at Marek's heart. She did not think the nightmare or even the scene appearing during his meditation could be serious. After all, it was only a dream. Only an illusion.

"No! Seriously! I don't feel stressed or under any pressure. I have a good wife, two beautiful children, and a booming business. What else can I ask for?" Marek said, and caressed Stephanie's shoulder with a smile.

"Marek, how well do you know your family story? If you look into it, do you think you might acquire some clue to your dream?" Stephanie asked him.

"Yep! That's right. I don't know much about my family history. I think I'm going to ask Mom this weekend. Will you and the boys come with me?"

"No, sorry. Unfortunately, we can't! You know Erik's friend, Mark? His birthday is this coming weekend. In fact, we're all invited to the party. You are coming, right?" Stephanie asked.

"You know I've never liked that kind of social activity, Stephanie. It's just too much polite talk about nothing or pretending to feel a way I'm not feeling. Why don't you take the boys to the party and I'll go to visit my mom?" Marek suggested with a hopeful look.

"Okay, do what you want. I suppose if you go, you'll just be bored anyway. But don't forget about the movie you promised to both boys," Stephanie said with a smile.

Just then Erik came into the kitchen.

"Erik, you must eat quickly. Your school bus will be here in 25 minutes," she said, turning her attention to her oldest son.

"Okay, Mom." Erik poured some cereal and milk into a bowl and started eating.

CHAPTER 2. SEARCHING FOR THE PAST

Because of his recurring dream, and because the funeral scene had appeared during his meditation, Marek now had many questions plaguing him, especially about his family history. That weekend he went to see his mom to find out if she could provide him with any answers.

FAMILY HISTORY

Marek's mom was waiting for him in the hallway when he stepped into his sister's home. "Mom, hi! How are you doing?"

"I thought I heard a car pull into the driveway," she said and moved forward to hug her son.

Marek's mom, Jana, 69, was living with his sister, Susan, in a suburb of Chicago. Susan, who was already 38, was not married, and mother and daughter made their home together quite comfortably. In 1955, when Jana was 25, she had married Frank Müller, a 32-year-old professor. A year later they had Marek, and then Susan followed in 1961. Unfortunately, while Frank was traveling in Europe for a lecture in 1965, he was killed in a car accident in Italy. He was only 42 years old at the time. His death was a huge shock to the young family. Marek had been 9 and Susan only 4. Fortunately, Marek's maternal grandma stepped in to help take care of her grandchildren so Jana could go to work and earn an income. Life was hard for them. After Frank's accident, they seldom had any connection with Frank's family, especially since they lived in Alaska.

Now Marek asked him mother, "Are you alone? Where is Susan?"

"She is at the school." Susan was a schoolteacher. "Today is the Sunday of her school's annual cook-out. Where are Stephanie and my two little angels?" his mother replied.

"Erik's friend has a birthday party today. You know I've never liked that kind of thing. So, I came to see you instead!" Marek told her.

Jana's face fell a little bit in disappointment since she missed her two grandsons very much.

"Well, anyway, this will give us time to talk," Marek said when he saw the look on her face. "I need to ask you about something important, Mom."

"What is so important then, Marek? You look very serious."

"Yes, Mom, it is serious. I need to know more about our family history – about your family history."

Marek then told her about his dreams. Since his father had died so young, and since Marek did not have much contact with his father's family, his only hope to learn about his history was from his mother's side. Jana looked at him with a smile. She was delighted to hear that Marek wanted to know her family history.

"Wait a minute," Jana said. She went to her bedroom and came back with a photo. The photo was very old and almost completely faded out.

"This photo is precious, Marek, so be careful with it. This was your grandpa's family in 1920. To have a photo taken at that time was a great luxury. It cost a lot of money in Czechoslovakia," she told him.

"The man in the center is your Great-Grandpa Thomas. He was 57 years old and next to him is your Great-Grandma Klara, who was 55 at that time. This is your Grandpa Pavel, his two brothers, Filip and Honza, and his sister, Anezka. Your grandpa was 33, the eldest child among four," she continued.

"Where is Grandma, Mom?" Marek asked.

"Your grandpa was not married yet when this picture was taken.

He married late in life. When he got married, he was already 35 years old. It was very rare in Czechoslovakia at that time, you know. He married two years later, after your great-grandpa's accident."

"What accident, Mom? No one has ever told me about an accident," Marek said.

"Your great-grandpa's family were poor farmers. Life was very difficult in the 1920s. Very unfortunately, your great-grandpa died in an accident just six months after this photo was taken." Marek quietly listened to his mother, completely focused on her story.

"How did he die, Mom?"

"It was a tragedy, a terrible accident! When his younger brother, your great-granduncle Patrik, was mounting a new horse for farming, the horse suddenly got out of control and ran straight toward your great-grandpa. The horse was young, only two years old. They had just purchased it from a neighbor. The horse kicked him in the ribs and broke two of them. He died a few days later. It was so sad. He was only 58 years old," she said with a mournful look on her face.

This sad news made Marek snap to attention. He looked more closely at the photo. The faces looked so familiar. Were these the faces he saw in the funeral in his dreams? He was not sure, especially since the faces in the old photo were vague and fading.

"After your great grandpa died, your grandpa, Pavel Damet, went to Paris to begin his new dream, a jewelry business. He realized that if he could bring jewelry – like the rhinestone, garnet, amber, sapphire, and agate jewelry being produced in Czech, Poland, and some other eastern European countries – if he could bring that jewelry to the western European countries, he could make a good fortune," she continued.

Marek absorbed this information with great interest and mounting excitement. When his mom fell silent, pondering her memories, he rushed to the kitchen and brought back a glass of water for her.

"It's okay, Mom, take your time. Don't get too emotional,"

Marek said. He regretted that he had not thought to bring a recorder along to record everything his mom was saying. After a minute, she resumed her story.

"His new business was a great success. Your grandpa went from being a poor farmer to a rich businessman. Within just three years, he had already earned a great fortune. He married your grandma, Darina, in March of 1923 when she was 27 years old.

"He also invited his two brothers, Filip and Honza, to join his business, once it had become successful. Naturally, since they were working so hard, his brothers became rich as well."

"Then what happened, Mom?" Marek asked anxiously.

Jana took a sip of water and paused a little bit.

"My mom, Darina, was pregnant the following year and had a baby boy they named Marek. This brought the whole family blessing and cheer. Unfortunately, Marek died of a lung infection when he was only two. To ease the sadness of losing the child, your grandpa put all of his efforts into the business. He had become one of the richest businessmen in Czechoslovakia. Because of his successful business, he had also become acquainted with many elegant royal families. Through them he learned about Russia's civil war from 1918 to 1922, and how the Communists had seized power.

"As you know, Communists do not allow people to have personal wealth or to own property. Your grandpa was afraid that Communism would soon spread to Czechoslovakia, and so he opened a bank account in a Swiss bank in 1928 to protect the money he had earned.

"Two years later, I was born. Your Uncle Franda was born two years after that. Finally, your second uncle, Lomy, was born another two years after Franda. That was 1932 and by then your grandpa was already 44 years old.

"In 1940, when I was 12, my mom told us the family story, especially about my grandpa's accident. She showed us this photo. After we saw it, she put it away in a safe place. It was so precious to her.

I believe I am the only one who can still remember this, since your uncles were too small at the time."

"Mom, I would like to take this photo to an expert to have it restored. They will increase the contrast and make it clearer. Would that be okay?" Marek asked.

"No! You may damage it. This is the only one!" Jana replied.

"They will not damage it. Please trust me, Mom! They will simply scan it and copy it into a computer. Then they will modify the scanned copy. You will get this original back, plus we will have as many copies of the restored picture as we want," Marek told her.

"Okay. But be careful. Promise you will bring it back to me," Jana said.

"Mom, I promise! But I have one more question. How did grandma acquire this photo?" Marek asked.

"When your Grandma Darina married your grandpa, he told her all about his family history. In addition, your Great-Grandma Klara was very fond of your grandma. They were just like mother and daughter. As I understand it, your grandma learned many things from her in-laws. Your grandpa kept this photo with him till he died."

"And how did he die, Mom?" Marek was very curious.

"Well, you already know that Germany occupied Czechoslovakia in 1938 and started WWII in 1939. At that time, when your grandpa recognized the situation was getting worse, he arranged for the whole family to escape to his best business friend, a Mr. Wagner in Austria. Since he had money and connections, he was able to bribe some high-ranking officers and get the family out to Austria smoothly before circumstances deteriorated further.

"Later, when Germany had gained complete control of Czechoslovakia, the Germans took all of the money from wealthy people, especially the Jews. Most of your grandpa's wealth was taken as well as your granduncles'. The family was becoming poor again and the war was rapidly expanding. If not for Grandpa's savings in the Swiss bank, they would not have been able to live in Austria comfortably." Jana paused a little bit, the solemn expression on her face shrouded in sadness.

"And then the Nazis began the Holocaust. From 1941 to 1945 they killed more than six million Jews. In one way, the family was so sad because of what was happening, and from learning that most of their friends and relatives were being killed. In another way, they felt blessed that they had escaped from this disaster. They hid in Austria until the war was over in 1945." Jana eyes turned red when she talked about this unbelievable human cataclysm.

"In just a year, your grandpa could see that the Russian Communists would soon control Czechoslovakia. He decided to take his family to France and escape from the Communists. He thought the Communists could be as bad, or even worse, than the Germans. That was in 1947. Your great-grandma was 82 already; your two granduncles were 57 and 55, and your grandaunt, 45. Since your great-grandma was so old already, she refused to run again. She would not believe that the Communists could be worse than the Germans. Your two granduncles and grandaunt also decided to stay and take care of their mom. So, it was only our family who left," Jana continued.

"I can't imagine the situation at that time. Everyone must have been in a panic," Marek said.

"Yes, all of us. I was 19. I was so scared! When we arrived in Paris, your grandpa was able to get some of his money from the Swiss bank account. So, our life was still not too bad. Unfortunately, in 1952 the Communists demanded your two granduncles surrender all of the wealth they had saved. When your granduncles refused, they were accused as betrayers of the Great Communist Party and executed. Your great-grandma was 87 years old and died of shock and sorrow a few days later." Jana eyes turned red again and this time she couldn't stop her tears from falling.

"A month later your grandpa learned about the misfortune and death of his mom and two brothers. He had a heart attack and died suddenly. He was only 65 years old," Jana continued.

"Did he pass the secret Swiss bank code to anyone?" Marek asked anxiously.

"Grandma said your grandpa did tell her, but she could not remember. It was a twenty-digit code. She did not expect her husband would die so suddenly," Jana replied.

"Mom, this story is amazing! I want to hear more, but it is getting too late now. Can we continue the story when we meet again? I promised Erik and Steffen that I would take them to a movie after they returned from their friend's birthday party. I'll bring this photo back when I come see you again, maybe next weekend, okay?"

Marek went to his sister's study and found a folder. He put the photo in the folder to keep it safe and protected. Then he hugged his mother good-bye and left.

CONNECTION

The next day Marek went to a photo shop. He returned to his office with the original photo and six extra printed copies. All of the copies had been enhanced and modified. Now, the contrast was better, and the facial expressions could be seen more clearly. He also stored digital copies of the original and the corrected photos in his computer. He kept looking at the faces in the picture and trying to connect them with the faces in his dreams. The more he looked, the more familiar it all felt.

It had been a while since Marek had had the nightmare, or had the scene appear during meditation. Marek began to think it might never happen again. But after work, when he returned home tired from his day, once he was relaxed all the images from the photo would appear in his mind. It was just like shadows hanging around his thoughts.

One morning he woke up around 1 a.m. and could not fall back to sleep. After tossing and turning for half an hour, he decided to meditate to calm his mind. Marek went to his study and sat down on the meditation cushion. With a few deep breaths, he was relaxed, and his mind was calm. He searched for the feeling of the semi-sleeping state that Embryonic Breathing Meditation leads to.

Gradually, he minimized his conscious mind's activities and soon intentional thought began to disappear. After 20 minutes, he entered the semi-sleeping state. It seemed that he was sleeping but his conscious mind was still there. Deeper and deeper his feeling went and more and more he reconnected with nature. Time was not important; his mind was in a neutral and calm state.

Suddenly, the image of the funeral appeared in his mind again. Strangely, this time the scene that appeared was crystal clear. He downplayed his conscious mind and directed it to see the faces of those present at the funeral. Now he could recognize them: his mother, two brothers, sister, and two uncles. There were also some others whom he could not recognize. He turned to look at his mom on his right and hugged her. She was sobbing.

"Pavel! You are the oldest boy in the family now. How are we going to survive? You will have to take care of the whole family," his mom said through her tears.

This brought his attention back to his conscious thinking, and he was awakened from the semi-sleeping state.

"Pavel! That was my grandpa's name! She called me Pavel! Am I my grandpa?" Marek sat in confusion and wondered.

FAMILY HISTORY CONTINUED

Sunday morning Marek took his wife and two boys back to visit his mom. He also brought the photos, both the original and copies. Jana was so excited to see her two grandchildren. She had known that they were coming and had already prepared a lot of food and dessert. Marek also brought a tape recorder this time. When they opened the door, Marek's mom was standing right next to it.

"I heard you parking. I have been waiting for you. Gosh! My two little angels! Give Grandma a hug." Jana squatted down and held out her arms to hug her grandkids. She was so happy to see them.

"Hi, Stephanie. Marek," she said once she stood up. "I have been waiting for this gathering for the whole week."

"Hi Mom! I've brought back your original photo, and these are copies. If you want more, I can always make copies from my computer," Marek said as he gave his mom the pictures. He kept four copies for himself.

"Wow! It is much clearer on the copies," Jana said with delight.

"Where is Susan? Is she home?" Stephanie asked.

"No! Finally, she has a boyfriend. I hope they love each other and get married. They went to the art museum. They said there was a special exhibition of oriental arts today. But I think they just don't want too many of us or too much bright light around to interfere with their privacy," Jana laughed.

After lunch, both boys were put down for a nap. Once they were settled, Marek and Stephanie went to sit in the living room with Jana. Actually, when Marek had arrived home last week, he had told Stephanie everything he had learned from his mom. The story had also piqued Stephanie's interest.

"So, Mom, can we continue the family history from last week?" Marek asked, taking the recorder out and turning it on.

"Yes, where were we? You know, I am not young anymore," Jana replied.

"You were talking about what had happened around Grandpa's death. It was so sad," Marek replied.

"Yes! Right! After your grandpa died in 1952, Grandma thought since we did not know much French - you know, I was 24 and your two uncles were 22 and 20 already - we might have a better chance to survive if we emigrated to America. Plus, Grandma was afraid that communism might spread all the way to France. America was probably the safest place at that time," Jana said.

"It was not until January 20th of 1954, we finally received approval from the American Embassy. We arrived in New York on March 2nd of 1954. We came by cargo ship, there were no commercial airplanes yet at the time. It took us about one month of sailing. I still remember the day we arrived very well. Grandma and the three of us were very excited and happy. It was a new hope for our future." Jana's face reflected a shining hope.

"Then what happened?" Stephanie asked eagerly. She was very curious about the family history.

"You know, it seems our family was always running from conflict and had never really settled down. I, and both your uncles, had never had a chance to go to college or university. All of us grew up during wartime. When the University of Chicago accepted Uncle Franda and Lomy and offered them scholarships, Grandma was so happy and could not refuse. These special scholarships were offered only to refugees at that time and there were so many people applying for them. That's why we moved to Chicago in June of 1954. We rented a cheap house near the University. We didn't have too much money. We had to be careful with every penny we spent." Jana picked up the cup in front of her and sipped a mouthful of tea.

"I found a librarian job at the University of Illinois in Chicago. Grandma couldn't speak English very well. You know she was 59 years old by then. She couldn't find any job except to baby-sit some professors' kids whenever she was called," Jana said.

Marek and Stephanie paid careful attention to the story.

"While I was working in the library, I got acquainted with your father. He visited the library almost every other day. I was 26 and Frank, your father, was 31 already. He was one of the young engineering professors teaching at the University of Illinois. Somehow, we fell in love with each other. We got married the following year, in 1955." Jana smiled at the memory.

"How did it happen? I mean, how did you fall in love with each other?" Marek asked curiously.

"After I'd been working about three months at the library, your father came to ask me some questions about Czechoslovakian history. Many people in the library knew I was from Czechoslovakia. Later, I figured out that he had just been looking for an excuse to talk to me. Anyway, he invited me out for dinner. Well! That was our first date." Jana smiled again.

"After that, we got together as often as we could. Lunch break, dinner, coffee, even just walking on the campus. In just a few months, we had fallen deeply in love already. What had happened was just like if a bolt of lightning hits you all of a sudden. He asked me to marry him after just ten months of dating." She paused a little, recalling the time in 1955.

"We got married on September 4th of 1955. It was a beautiful sunny day. We did not have a big party. There were eight of your father's family that flew in from Alaska. You know your father was from Alaska. Actually, that was the first time I met his parents and relatives. It was strange at first, but we got acquainted very fast.

"After that, your father and I went to Alaska to see his family just one time. I wanted to visit with them, but I was also interested in seeing Alaska. Actually, I was four months pregnant with you already. We were so happy, and life was great. After you were born, we seldom traveled. You know it's not easy traveling with small kids." Jana looked at Marek with a big smile.

"I have always been curious about my first name. Marek. It's not a common American name. Where is it from, Mom?" Marek asked.

"Actually, Marek was also your first uncle's name, remember? Grandma's first child who died young at 2? When I was pregnant, my mom asked me if we could name you Marek if you were a boy, since she missed her first born so much. Naturally, both Frank and I agreed," Jana explained.

"Now I understand where my first name came from. My friends have always been curious about it," Marek said.

"Then what happened?" Stephanie asked.

"Yes! One thing I should tell you! The night before your father and

I got married, Grandma brought me to her room. She took a ring from a box that she always kept with her. She told me that the ring was given to her by her mom when she married your grandpa. She said in the box there were many memories, both good and bad. You know, after that, you were born the next year and then Susan in 1961," Jana said.

Now the story had reached a time that Marek knew better since it was not so very long ago.

"I do know. After that came the big disaster when father died in Italy in 1965. I can never forget that time. When the news arrived at home, I was 9 and Susan was only 5. I remember it very well, Mom! You were so sad! You sobbed, and hugged Susan and me so tightly. It was the unhappiest day of my life. Grandma was also very sad. It seems our family has a lot of sorrowful memories in our past," Marek said.

"Yes. But I had to stay strong in order to survive, you know. I still had two kids and my mom to look after. I kept reminding myself that I must be tough. After I married your dad and had the two of you, I stopped working. But after your father died, I needed to find a job again. I was lucky. Through your father's professor friends, I was again able to get a job as a librarian. It did not pay a lot, but it was enough for us to survive. And you know Grandma was the one who took care of you while I was working."

"I remember. Grandma was always telling us old stories, but she never mentioned any sad things. She always made us laugh," Marek said.

"When you were 18, you entered Babson College. Fortunately, you were able to receive a scholarship from Babson; otherwise, I would not have been able to send you to such an expensive private business college. Grandma was already 78 by then. Your sister was still in high school, but she was old enough that she no longer needed your grandma to take care of her."

"What happened then?" Stephanie asked curiously. She was

completely engrossed in Jana's detailed reciting of Marek's family history, something that Marek seldom talked about.

"When Marek graduated in 1978, I was so happy. He was an honor student and had graduated with high grades. Immediately, a few companies offered him jobs. It was a big decision, but in the end, he chose an import/export company near Chicago so we could all be together. He began to bring home an income and help support the family. It was a great relief to me that Marek was able to help pay his sister's way through college, Stephanie. At that time Marek was almost 23 and Susan was only 18.

"Our financial situation continued to improve as Marek showed he had a real talent for his job. Unfortunately, his grandma, Darina Damet, passed away in 1983 at the age of 88. You know it was rare to live to be so old at that time. She was a good and strong woman," Jana recounted fondly.

"I wish I had met her before she died. Marek and I didn't get married until '88," Stephanie said.

"And then, after eight years of working for someone else, Marek decided to start his own company. So, he resigned from his job and opened up Müller's Import & Export, Inc., turning it into the fine company that it is now. I don't know what he does or how he does it. He just seems to have a natural flair for the import/export business. Usually it would take many more years of experience than Marek had at the time to start up your own company, much less to have it reach the level of success that he has achieved. Right from the start he was especially talented trading in jewelry, diamonds, and precious stones. His old company manager told me once that Marek was a natural born talent at this kind of business," Jana concluded.

These last comments in particular captured Marek's attention. His grandpa had also been in the import/export business and had also been an expert in precious stones. "Are my abilities somehow the benefit of a genetic memory from my grandpa?" he wondered.

"Will I be able to access this memory through meditation?" He was very curious.

CHAPTER 3. REACHING THE OTHER WORLD

At the beginning of summertime in 1999, Marek's mind was over-flowing with questions about meditation.

Questions like, "Is my spirit my grandpa's? Am I the reincarnation of my grandpa? Or is it just some kind of memory held in my genes and passed down to me?"

Or, "Will I be able to control my dreams?"

And, "How can I access all of the genetic memory through medi-tation?"

The more Marek thought about these questions, the more curious he became and the more frustrated he was that he did not have the answers. He decided to talk to his friend Steve again. Nearly a year had passed since they had had their conversation about meditation. Marek picked up the phone and dialed Steve's number.

"Hi, Steve! Say, it's been a while. How is your family?"

"Hello, Marek! It's you! I was just thinking about you a couple of days ago after my meditation. I was wondering how your meditation is coming. Any progress?" Steve replied.

"Gosh! Are you psychic? How do you know why I'm calling you?" Marek laughed.

"Just a lucky guess. Usually, you don't call me, I call you, remem-ber?"

"True," Marek laughed again. "I was wondering if you might be able to come to my family's cook-out this July 4th? It's a Sunday, and we have Monday off, so, we can have a big celebration. If you come, I have a few meditation questions that I need to ask you."

"I'm not sure Marek. My son Kevin will be with me the July 4th weekend. It's my turn to take care of him over the holiday. My ex-wife and her boyfriend are going to Europe on vacation."

"That's great! You can bring Kevin along. How old is he now? Nine, right? It will be great. Erik and Steffen would love to play with him. Kevin can be a big brother to my boys," Marek said.

"Well, okay. We'll be there at noon. Lunch and dinner? Right?" Steve joked.

"No sweat! There'll be plenty of food. Both my mom and Stephanie's mom will be here. When they are here together, there is always lots of delicious food."

"I can't wait! See you this weekend," Steve said.

* * *

On July 4, Steve brought Kevin to Marek's home around 11:30 in the morning. Marek's mom, Stephanie's mom, and Marek's sister, Susan, were there already. Steve went to help Marek at the grill, while the grandmas, Susan, and Stephanie were busy in the kitchen preparing salad and desserts. The kids were playing in the backyard. It was a beautiful day; the best weather for a cookout.

"So, what questions do you have?" Steve asked as soon as he greeted Marek at the grill.

"Let's talk about it after lunch. I cannot cook and think at the same time. These thoughts are too profound for me. I need a calm and quiet environment to contemplate them. How about we retreat to my study this afternoon, maybe around 2:30 when everyone is tired and needing a rest? Does that sound okay?" Marek suggested.

"Sure. You sound very serious." Steve said.

"To me, yes, this is very serious. I need to know the answers," Marek replied.

After lunch, when the tired kids were sent to the bedrooms for a nap and the women in the house settled in the living room to talk, Marek and Steve went to the study. Once they were seated, Marek told Steve about the scene that kept recurring in his dreams and meditation.

"I don't know how this happens. And why does it happen?" Marek asked.

"Actually, no scientist yet is able to explain how and why we have dreams. All they say is that dreams may be triggered from either our conscious mind or subconscious mind," Steve said.

"I know this already, but how about genetic memory? Can genetic memory trigger dreams, Steve?" Marek asked.

"It's possible. As I understand it, genetic memory is the memory that is passed down to descendants from generation to generation. This memory is generated by occurrences that were repetitious in the past, or by an event that was traumatizing or astonishing and therefore stuck in your ancestor's subconscious mind for a long period of time. That is why animals are able to find water, suck milk, or migrate from place to place without being taught. You may say it is animal instinct. Naturally, we humans also have these genetic memories, although we tend to be unaware of them or to ignore them," Steve explained.

"How are these memories recorded in our mind? And where?"

"Genetic memory is stored in the limbic system of the head. You know, the center of the head. Though there are no brain cells there, it has memory. As I said, these memories were initiated by repeated events in past lives or some shocking incident that happened in the past and stuck in the subconscious mind," Steve said.

"If this is the case, then we can analyze current thinking or behaviors based on past human history. Right?" Marek asked.

"Theoretically, yes, that's true," Steve replied.

"But if we look at human history, it is completely steeped in defeating and subjugating other people. In killing, violence, slavery, and rape," Marek said.

"That is why all the movies, computer games or novels related to these subjects sell. These are in our blood. Usually, we hide these dark sides of our subconscious feelings behind our masks. You know, we call it privacy. You should understand that we also have the bright side of genetic memories such as love, compassion, kindness, harmony, peace, and justice. Our dark side makes us excited and violent while the bright side makes us peaceful, calm, and harmonized. From these, our spirits evolved. One is Yang and the other is Yin, as the Chinese say."

"So, what I have seen in my dreams was from my genetic memory, right?" Marek asked curiously.

"It's possible. Since you know it was not from your conscious mind it has to be related to your subconscious mind. As I mentioned, the subconscious mind also originates in the limbic system."

"Gosh! You are amazing, Steve! You've been a great help with my mystery," Marek said.

"Remember what I told you about that Embryonic Breathing Meditation book last year? It's all in there," Steve told him.

"I did purchase some books and DVDs about Embryonic Breathing Meditation. I read, watched, pondered them, and practiced. But I still have a lot of questions. For instance, about the two poles of a human body, or the two dimensions of the universe. I wonder, if this meditation is so important in Chinese meditation, how come there isn't much information on it available?"

"Well, Embryonic Breathing Meditation has been a well-kept secret in Chinese monasteries for a long time. It was not until the 1980s that these secrets were revealed to the general public. Actually, the best way to learn about it is through participating in seminars. Speaking of which, I am again going to some seminars next month in northern California. Since you have so many questions, why don't you come with me? There are still a few openings. We'll have a great time! You know, we haven't gotten together as much as we used to when we were in high school," Steve said.

"I'm sorry, but I can't, Steve. Honestly, I am very interested. But summertime is the time of year when I travel for business. If I don't get supplies ordered for the Christmas season, it will mean a huge loss of business." Marek looked at Steve with regret.

"Ha, ha! You are in a different matrix from me," Steve responded. "I thought you had all the freedom in your job that I could never have. Please don't worry, my pal. You actually can visit Master Tang at the center anytime. The center is always open to the public."

"If you don't mind, I would like to continue our conversation though. You are not only my best friend but also the best teacher," Marek said, since he wanted to learn as much as he could from Steve.

"Okay! Okay! Don't flatter me. Just tell me what you want to know," Steve laughed.

"So how do you reach this genetic memory in your meditation?" Marek asked.

"Once you have reached a profound meditative state, it will be kind of like you are hypnotized except your conscious mind is still there to govern your thinking instead of being controlled by a hypnotist. Often, through this subconscious feeling, you will be able to travel without the limitation or restriction of time and space," Steve continued.

"What do you mean that you are able to travel without the limitation or restriction of time and space?" Marek asked.

"Well, you know. From the Chinese Yi Jing. I mean the ancient classic, The Book of Change, there are two spaces or two worlds co-existing in nature: a material world called Yang World and a spiritual world called Yin World."

Steve tried to explain further what he had learned from Chinese culture, especially about spiritual cultivation.

"Since we humans were created and developed in these two worlds, we also have two lives in our body, a physical life and a spiritual life."

"I agree with you on that, Steve. I have always believed and felt that we have two lives in our body, physical and spiritual. Somehow, through the material sciences we have come to understand the material world to a profound level, but we still don't have a clear idea about the spiritual world," Marek said.

"That's correct, Marek. You know you are smart!" Steve confirmed, nodding his head and looking at Marek. "Actually, though, there is no one who is able to explain the spiritual world scientifically today. As I said before, our science is still in its infant stage. However, though we still don't know anything about the spiritual world, yet all cultures throughout the world have come to a realization that each person has a physical life and a spiritual life.

"Have you ever read the *Dao De Jing* by Lao Zi? You know it is the second most popular book after the Bible and has been translated into just as many languages. Actually, The *Dao De Jing* talks about these two worlds, dimensions, spaces, or whatever you call it. Roughly speaking, Dao is the spiritual world and De is the material world. De is the manifestation of the Dao," Steve continued.

"I read a *Dao De Jing* translation. I didn't see much information about the spiritual world though. Most of it was talking about the cultivation of personal temperament and deed. Also, a big part of it talked about how to rule a country," Marek argued.

"Yes, I know. That's because scholars instead of Qigong practitioners did almost all of the interpretations and translations in the past. You know, Lao Zi was not a ruler but a Qigong practitioner. What he did was apply the principles and rules of Qigong self-regulation and cultivation to politics. When Dao is applied to a human body, it is the mind or thinking and De is the actions or behaviors manifested from thinking. Since 1922, scientists have discovered that there is another world consisting of what they call 'dark energy' or 'dark matter.' When they tried to calculate the actions of stars using the knowledge they had at the time, it did not make sense. Since there is gravitational force between materials, the universe should be shrinking due to that gravitational force. However, from what scientists have observed, the universe is actually expanding at the speed of light.

Finally, scientists discovered that if they assumed there was dark matter or energy coexisting with our material world, and if this dark matter is anti-gravitational, then all their calculations became accurate. In this dark energy dimension, time does not have meaning since the energy can be transmitted from one end of the universe to the other instantly," Steve explained.

"All right. Now I think I know much more clearly why we have two lives, a physical life and a spiritual life, in our bodies. As you said, since we humans were developed in these two dimensions, so we also have two lives?" Marek asked.

"Bingo! You know, morality in Chinese society is called Dao-De and means thinking and behavior. Dao is the thinking and De is the behavior," Steve said.

"See if I am right, Steve. If the mind is the Dao that belongs to the dark matter dimension, then there is no time or space restriction in our mind, right? That is why our mind can travel to the past and future instantly. Not only that, but our mind is also able to travel to any place in this universe without delay."

"Yes, Marek, you are correct. You are smart and able to link all these concepts together."

This discussion was of enormous interest to Marek. He had always been amazed by oriental cultures such as the Indian, Japanese, and Chinese. But he had never had a chance to work on gaining a deeper understanding of any of them other than through his Indian Yoga practice.

"But you know, the mind or thinking is not the same as spirit," Marek said. "This makes me confused. Furthermore, how is Embryonic Breathing Meditation related to any of this?" he asked.

"You see? We have two minds! Our conscious mind and our subconscious mind. Our conscious mind is run by our brain and produces our thoughts. Once we think, we play tricks on ourselves and lie to ourselves. We 'rationalize.' From our conscious mind we have generated a human matrix that is full of dogmas and traditions that can put us into physical and spiritual slavery. Into bondage, or abuse. However, your subconscious mind that is fostered in the limbic system at the center of your head, is more truthful. Though the limbic system is not the source of your thinking, it has memory. This memory includes genetic memory or subconscious routines that were developed from repetition in the past."

"So, Embryonic Breathing Meditation teaches you how to minimize the actions of your conscious mind and allow the subconscious mind and feeling to be developed. Is this what you're saying? Is that right?" Marek asked.

"Yes! The way of awakening your subconscious mind is through downplaying your conscious mind," Steve confirmed.

"Okay. Now tell me, what is the basic concept or theory in this training? Can you explain that to me, Steve?" Marek asked.

"Well, I can try from what I have learned so far. But I am not an expert or a Jedi yet! You know, I am just a beginner and have only practiced for a few years," Steve replied.

"Well, try your best! Treat me as your student and you can try to brainwash or convince me," Marek joked with a laugh.

"Okay. Basically, there are only a few key concepts that build the foundation of Embryonic Breathing Meditation. First, you must know what the cavities are," Steve said.

"You mean cavities, like in teeth? What are you talking about?"

"Be serious, Marek. There are two kinds of cavities defined in Chinese medicine and Qigong. First, cavities are the energy holes where acupuncturists insert the needles into your skin so the Qi circulation in Qi channels can be corrected or regulated. You know, according to Dr. Robert Becker's book, 'The Body Electric', acupuncture cavities are actually the higher electrically conductive areas on the skin. Through these cavities, the needle will be able to stimulate the Qi's circulation in Qi channels, called meridians."

"Now I understand why Qi is most likely the bioelectricity circulating in our bodies. I remember you mentioned that last year," Marek said.

"That's the reason that cavities are more sensitive than other areas, since Qi circulation is more abundant in these areas. Cavities are just like the windows of a house. They allow Qi to breath between the inside and the outside of the body. Through these windows, an acupuncturist is able to access the main Qi streams and adjust them."

"What about the other kind of cavities?" Marek asked.

"The other kind is a Qi or energy center where energy is emitted and collected. You know that the center of a sphere is the energy center. From this center, energy can be emitted and collected. If you have a space shaped like an ellipse, then..."

Marek interrupted, "Then you have two Qi centers, right? I know this from physics." Marek laughed.

"Yes, you are right. Actually, there is always at least one or more Qi centers in various shapes of spaces. These energy centers are what those Chinese Fengshui masters look for. That is because, if you are in these centers, you will receive the Qi and resonate within the space effectively. For example, if you meditate at the center of a sphere, you will find the energy is strong. Even if you just make a tiny sound, you will vibrate the entire space and hear all of that sound energy bounced back to you," Steve explained.

"That means if two people are meditating at the two centers or poles of an elliptical space, they should be able to communicate with each other much more easily, right?" Marek said, showing he understood the point that Steve was trying to explain.

"Yes!"

"But what does 'Fengshui' mean? I have never heard of it," Marek asked.

"Feng means wind and Shui is water. They refer to a setting that is related to the wind's blow and to the existence of water. There is a profession in China since ancient times that specializes in searching for these energy centers. Actually, those who practice Fengshui are not just looking for the energy centers but also study their relationship with how the wind blows and whether there is some water nearby. You know, wind and water are two other important elements that affect the energy of a place."

"Now tell me how these things relate to the two poles of a human body. You mentioned two human poles a couple of times, but I still don't have a good idea of how that works," Marek probed.

"Okay. You know, scientists have already confirmed that every one of our cells has two poles, Yin and Yang, or negative and positive charges. That's why each cell is a tiny battery that can store energy charges or bioelectricity. When a cell divides, new cells will be produced until the entire body is constructed. Once the body is completely constructed, we then also have two poles in our body."

"You'll have to explain more; I'm just not sure," Marek said.

"Okay. First, can you tell me what the difference is between an embryo and a fetus?" Steve questioned Marek.

"I don't know. I thought they were the same. Aren't they?"

"Of course not. That is why there are two different names. A human embryo is when the egg is fertilized and grows to be eight weeks old. It is commonly called a pea or a bean since it is shaped like a bean, you know? Like an ellipse. In this stage, there are no arms or legs visible yet. This is how the two human poles are first formed. One is at the center of your head and the other is at the center of your physical body where your guts are. These two centers are connected by the spinal cord. After eight weeks of pregnancy, it is then called a fetus since you can see the development of arms and legs.

"By the way, the guts are called the second brain in science. Dr. Michael Gershon announced it January 23rd of 1996. And though there are two brains in our body, since they are connected by the spinal cord, in function, there is only one. This is because the spinal cord is constructed from highly electrically conductive tissues. These two poles synchronize with each other simultaneously without any kind of signal delay."

Marek was starting to realize just how much more easily Steve was able to understand this was because of his training as a physicist.

"In Chinese Qigong concepts, the top brain is called Upper Dan Tian and means Upper Elixir Field, while the lower brain is called Lower Dan Tian or Lower Elixir Field. Between them, there is a vessel called Thrusting Vessel which connects these two poles. This vessel is what western science calls the 'spinal cord.' The Upper Dan Tian is the source of your thinking and stores memories, while the Lower Dan Tian stores memories only. What Qigong practitioners have experienced over the last couple of thousand years is that the top brain is able to control the energy's or Qi's manifestation, while the lower brain is able to store the energy or Qi to an abundant level. Conclusively, the top brain governs the quality of energy's manifestation while the lower brain is the battery that stores and supplies the Qi's quantity. You know, to keep our life healthy, we need to know both how to store energy to an abundant level and how to consume it efficiently," Steve continued.

"Amazing! That implies that our entire body actually is a big battery since there are two poles. Right?" Marek said.

"Exactly. These two poles are the spiritual and energy centers that govern the energy's storage and manifestation in your entire body. From these two poles, countless small cell batteries are derived. The beginning of Embryonic Breathing Meditation is to find or feel these two centers: the spirit center and the energy center. From these two centers, you learn how to focus subconsciously and store your Qi to an abundant level," Steve replied.

"Now my mind is clearer. After I read the book and watched the DVD, I was still confused. But you are telling me that in order to keep healthy and live a long life, we must recognize these two poles and know how to govern them. Am I right?" Marek said.

"Yep! In Embryonic Breathing Meditation practice, first you must learn how to minimize the actions of your conscious mind. As I've said before, once our conscious mind is engaged, we play tricks and lie to ourselves. The conscious mind makes us put a mask on our face so that we present a false self to the world. Through our conscious mind, we try to hide our dark side by using dignity, glory, honor, loyalty, and pride to decorate the appearance of the mask. As a result of these dogmas we kill, conquer, enslave, or rape to enforce the false façade. The first step of spiritual cultivation is taking your mask off and facing the real you behind the mask. This step is called 'self-recognition.' Only if you are able to release yourself from this dogmatic bondage will your subconscious mind be free and able to grow. You know, as I have said a few times, the subconscious mind is more truthful and is able to access your natural spirit. When your mind is at the limbic system, you will conserve your energy," Steve continued.

"I thought you said the energy center is in the lower brain," Marek said.

"Yes, it is. But you see, once you are able to minimize your thinking and allow your subconscious mind to wake up, your mind will be calm and peaceful. Your conscious mind will only lead you to thoughts of chaos, confusions, and emotions. When this happens, the Qi will be led away for manifestation. Remember, the top spiritual center and the lower energy center correspond with each other simultaneously. As I said earlier, though there are two, in function there is only one. That means when the top is calm and peaceful, energy will be able to stay at the lower center for storage."

"What happens once you are able to minimize your conscious mind and wake up your subconscious mind?" Marek asked.

"Then you are facing the truth of yourself. Those dogmas or spiritual bonds hidden behind your mask will be downplayed," Steve replied.

"That means you are also able to feel or sense a lot of things stored in your genetic memory. Right?" Marek asked further.

"Very good, Marek!" Steve appraised.

"Then what? What would the next step be, Steve?" Marek was getting more excited the more he was able to comprehend what Steve said. Now, he was sure that the scene appearing in his dreams and meditation was subconsciously coming from his genetic memory.

"You have to find the physical center. You know, the center of gravity in your body. The center between the top of your pelvis bones. Remember what I told you last year? If your mind cannot recognize or register where the energy center is, how can you lead the energy there and store it? That's why recognition of the energy center with your mind is the second step," Steve said.

"After that, then you synchronize the upper and lower centers so they are able to harmonize with each other smoothly. You told me that last year. Remember? But, why do I need to synchronize them? Don't they synchronize with each other simultaneously and automatically?" Marek asked.

"As a beginner, no! You know the top center controls the energy's manifestation while the lower center stores and supplies the energy. That means the top center functions as a steering wheel while the lower center acts as the wheels. To a new driver, it is necessary for him to learn how to develop the feel of using the steering wheel to control the wheels so the car can go straight or move as he wishes. This feeling takes time to develop. It is the same in Embryonic Breathing. It takes time to synchronize and harmonize these two poles smoothly and naturally," Steve replied.

"Only then will you be able to bring your mind down to the lower center. That means unifying the spirit and the energy at a single point. It is called 'the unification of mother and son.' Son is the spirit and Mother is the energy or Qi. When this happens, it is called 'embracing singularity.'"

"I remember Chapter 10 of the *Dao De Jing* mentions this. If I remember it correctly, it says, 'When bearing and managing the vital spirit and embracing singularity, can it be not separated?' Is this what that means?" Marek asked. He had read the *Dao De Jing* many times. He had been very attracted to the philosophical inside.

"Wow! Yes, it is! I did not know you were so familiar with the *Dao De Jing*. When your spirit and energy are united, you are returning to the beginning of life, you know, as an embryo. Once you have reached a profound stage in this practice, you are like an infant just born; soft, natural, truthful, simple, and innocent. This is the passageway to reconnecting your spirit with nature. This stage is called 'unification of heaven and human.' Remember this sentence in Chapter 10? It says, 'When concentrating the Qi to reach its softness, can it be as (soft as) a baby?'"

"Yes, I remember. It's starting to sound like many chapters in the *Dao De Jing* are talking about Embryonic Breathing Meditation. Now that I understand the theory, it sounds easy to do. Why aren't there more people who know this and practice it?" Marek asked.

"There are a few reasons. First, as I mentioned earlier, almost all documents related to Embryonic Breathing Meditation were hidden in Chinese Buddhist and Daoist monasteries. It wasn't until the 1980s that all of these documents were revealed to laymen society. Second, though there were many, many documents developed over the last two thousand years, each one of them could only provide you a small piece of information. You know, there wasn't clear theoretical or scientific support in ancient times. It would be just as if you didn't know where New York City was, and there was no map to guide you. All you would know is that New York City exists. Just like that, many people were looking for New York City without a map. It took countless people searching for two thousand years to find New York City. Finally, someone found it and wrote down his experience as a guide to others who were searching. It's the same with Embryonic Breathing Meditation. Each document can provide us only a small part of the entire map. Once you put all the parts together, actually, it is very simple and clear.

"Now, the map is complete, and it provides us a passageway to our future spiritual evolution. Embryonic Breathing Meditation is the crucial key to reach this goal. However, you should understand that even though the map is provided; that does not mean the goal is easy to reach. It will be a long journey of walking on foot from Chicago to

New York City. There is no car or airplane available for this kind of spiritual cultivation. To reach the goal, a person needs to conquer himself and hold himself to a higher discipline, step by step by step," Steve concluded.

"Then how is Embryonic Breathing Meditation connected with genetic memory?" Marek asked, bringing the conversation back around to his chief concern.

"All I know is that when your subconscious mind is awakened, it can reconnect with the other world. I don't know very much about the theory behind this. We are just getting into the 'unification of heaven and human' in the seminar. I think it will be discussed next month at the California seminars," Steve said.

"What do you mean 'the other world'?" Marek asked anxiously.

"Remember what I said earlier? From the Chinese Yi Jing, The Book of Change, written nearly 4,000 years ago? It says there are two dimensions or spaces co-existing in this nature. One is called 'Yin space' or spiritual space and the other is called 'Yang space' or material space. Though there are two spaces, in function it is only one since these two spaces or poles correspond with each other synchronously. Once you have reached the final stage of Embryonic Breathing Meditation, you will have returned your life to the beginning and you should be able to feel or sense the other world. This was also written in the Dao De Jing. That's all I know so far. If you wish to know more, you will have to go see Master Tang and ask him yourself," Steve said, matter-of-factly.

Since Steve could not provide any more details, their discussion came to an end. Besides, the kids had just woken up from their nap and were starting to get noisy again. In any event, it would take a long time for Marek to ponder and digest the information he had just received from Steve.

CHAPTER 4. A TRIP

TRIP PROPOSAL

While those who had invested in the stock market before 1999 were enjoying the amazing growth of their stock values, most of them did not realize that the almost out of control growth was only a bubble that would eventually burst. The value of stocks in Marek's company, Müller's Important & Export, Inc., had also reached sky high by the end of 1999. Everyone was excited and expected values to go even higher. Some people even quit their jobs and spent all their time playing the stock exchange. They believed they could make a bigger fortune that way than by just working hard.

At the beginning of December, Marek turned to Stephanie while they were eating dinner with their family.

"Stephanie, I think we would make a great deal of money if we traded in all our stocks - including our outside investments and our own company stocks – and turned it all into cash," he said.

"I'm also thinking, maybe we could sell just some and buy a bigger house. This one is getting to be a little too small now that Erik and Steffen are bigger. They each need to have their own room," Marek continued.

"Yes! I was thinking about that too. And, I would really like it if we could take a vacation," Stephanie said.

"I'd like to take a vacation to Europe. I'd especially like to visit Czechoslovakia where my parents came from. I bet my mom would like to go with us if we go," Marek said with a grin.

"Then let's go!" Stephanie replied. "Erik and Steffen are old enough to travel with us, especially if your mom is along to help take care of them."

"Should we sell some stock do you think, or should we use our savings, Stephanie?"

"Marek! Our savings are for emergencies. I think we should just sell some of the stock we own in outside companies. What do you think? We wouldn't have to sell much. The trip won't cost so much that we wouldn't be able to buy a new house, right?" Stephanie laughed happily. It looked like there was hope they were going to visit Europe soon.

"Okay. I think I'll ask Uncle Franda and Lomy if they also want to go. When they left Czechoslovakia, they were 17 and 15. My mom was 19. They all still have memories of Czechoslovakia. I expect they miss it too."

"I thought Uncle Franda visited Czechoslovakia six years ago?"

"Yes, I remember that. Once he got back, he talked to Mom for an entire hour about the trip. But I believe he would like to go again, especially if he's going together with Mom and Uncle Lomy."

"I'm sure you're right about that. Wow! It's so exciting to think about, Marek! When can we go?" Stephanie asked.

"If we go, it has to be after Christmas but before New Year's. You know I'll be busy at work again right after the New Year."

The next morning, Marek contacted his stock broker and sold some of his peak stock for a total of around $15,000, enough for his family to travel comfortably for one week.

The following weekend, when his whole family was visiting Jana again, Marek brought up the idea of the trip.

"Mom, Stephanie and I are thinking of taking a short vacation to the Czech Republic after Christmas. I was wondering if you would like to go with us?"

"What did you say? Is it true? Would I like to go? Listen, Marek. I have missed Czechoslovakia so much the last 52 years since we left.

After we immigrated to America, we were so poor for a long time. Later, between your father's accident and the hardship we had, it just wasn't possible to go back, especially while the Communists were still controlling the country. When Czechoslovakia separated from Communist Russia in 1989, I was so happy and hoped we could go back to visit. But then you started your own business and were so busy. And, of course, after that you had gotten married to Stephanie and had my two small angels! I was afraid to ask you if we could go back to visit. Oh, Marek! Don't you know how much I want to go? Most of our relatives are still there, you know. I have not seen your grand aunts and uncles since 1947 and have not met the new generation at all!"

"Mom, you know that Czechoslovakia was divided into two countries, Czech Republic and Slovakia on January 1, 1993. Now, which country was our home before?"

"Of course, I know about the separation. Our family is on the Czech side. Uncle Franda told me on the phone. He visited Czech six years ago when Czechoslovakia divided. He was so excited that finally Czech had been freed from Russian's control."

"Do you think Uncle Franda might want to go again? I believe Uncle Lomy would like to go since, like you, he has not been back there for so many years."

"Let's call them and ask them. If we all go, it would be an unforgettable trip and reunion. I am so excited, Marek!"

Jana immediately picked up the phone and dialed Franda's number first, since he was the older one.

"Hi, Franda. How are you doing?"

"Very good, Jana. It is you! We have not talked for a few months already. Gosh! Time passes so fast. Now, every second counts for us. We are old, Jana. So, tell me what has happened. Is Susan finally getting married?" Franda joked.

"I wish it was true. But there is other exciting news that I want to talk to you about. Marek is proposing that we all go to visit Czech right after Christmas. I was wondering if you might want to go. It will be so great if you do."

"Naturally. After my last visit, with all the great hospitality I received from our old relatives, naturally I want to go again. I am retired and have a lot of time now. Actually, I miss our old times very much. Tell me again, when will we leave and return?"

"It will be right after Christmas and return at the beginning of next year. I will also call Lomy and see if he wants to go."

"I believe he will. He was so envious about my last visit. I believe he'll want to go for sure."

"Okay! I'll contact him right after we hang up."

"Hi! Lomy. My little baby brother! How are you doing?" Jana said when Lomy picked up the phone.

"Jana, it is you! Come on, I am not a baby anymore and I am not little. What's up?" He and Jana had been very close since they were children. They always joked with each other.

"Do you miss Czechoslovakia? Do you want to go visit?"

"Are you kidding? I was so jealous when Franda went last time! Are we going?"

"Yes. Marek proposes we go. He is very anxious to visit. It will be Marek's family, you, and Franda."

"Is Susan going?"

"I don't think so since she has been so busy with her boyfriend, Kyle. I believe they want to spend time together alone, especially over the holiday."

"Okay! Count me in. I am excited already. You know, it has been a long, long time."

VISITING CZECH

On December 26 Uncle Franda flew to Chicago to meet everyone. Then they took off together on December 27, flying first to Paris and then on to the Czech Republic. Once they had landed at Prague Airport, two cousins of Jana's, Milan and Martin, and their sons, came with two cars to pick everyone up. They were welcomed warmly with many hugs and happy greetings. Jana and Lomy had not seen their cousins since they left Czechoslovakia in 1947. They were all very excited to see each other.

Marek could understand some of the Western Slavic his relatives were speaking, but not completely. However, judging by Jana's facial expression, he could tell how very happy they all were to see each other again. Marek's family was brought from the airport to a hotel downtown, since there was not enough space for their cousins to host so many visitors in their homes. That evening, there was a welcome feast for all of them at one cousin's house. They talked about how many friends or relatives had survived the Nazi Holocaust. They also talked about what life was like after the Communists took over. Not everything their cousins told them was information Franda, Jana, and Lomy had known about, even though they had stayed current with events by reading about them in newspapers at the time. The whole group was happy to be together, even as they shared their sad past experiences.

Marek and his family were faced with so many new and young faces that they had never met. However, through their awkward English, and Marek's poor Western Slavic, somehow, they managed to communicate with each other.

During dinner Marek asked his mother, "Mom! Can you ask my uncles if they can take us to Great-Grandpa's grave? I would like to go there and show my respect."

Actually, he wanted to see if the cemetery looked the same as the one he had seen in his dreams. But he did not want to explain that to the whole family as they might just laugh at him. He took three copies of the old photos of his great-grandpa's family from his briefcase, two for his two great-uncles' families and one for his great-aunt's.

"Mom, I brought three copies of the family picture for them. I didn't know if they had any copies themselves?" Marek looked at his mom and handed photos to her.

Jana was very excited since she didn't know Marek had brought the photos. They would be so precious to her relatives. She talked to her oldest cousin, Milan, who was the son of her oldest uncle, Filip. She still remembered that Communists had killed both Uncle Filip and Uncle Honza back in 1952. She gave Milan the three photos and told him that if they needed more, they could make copies from these. She also talked to him for a few minutes about the possibility of visiting Great-grandpa's cemetery. After that, she turned her head to Marek.

"Marek, Uncle Milan said he would arrange it, maybe for this Thursday. They have already arranged some sightseeing tours for us for the next two days. His son and Uncle Martin's son are available to show us around. They took time off from their work till next Sunday. And then we leave next Tuesday. This visit is too short! I wish I could stay longer. We have to come back again soon before I get too old to walk," Jana said with a laugh.

VISITING THE GRAVE

Though the ground was covered by snow, they were lucky that it was sunny the following two days. The weather was a little bit chilly and windy, but at least it was not raining or snowing. Thursday's weather, on the other hand, would be gloomy with the possibility of snow.

Over the next two days they visited famous sights such as the Old Town where there were many beautiful historic buildings and cultural places. They also visited the Astronomical Clock, famous St. Vitus Cathedral, and Lobkowicz Palace. After two days of sightseeing, everyone was feeling tired especially Jana, Franda, Lomy, and the two little ones.

"People have said Prague is the most beautiful city in the world. How true it is! It's full of history and culture. It would take probably an entire month to see everything. I will have to come back again, definitely," Marek thought when they were in the car returning to their hotel Wednesday night.

Thursday morning at 9 a.m., Milan and Martin again came with their sons in the cars. Jana, Franda, Lomy and Marek were ready to go but Marek's sons, Erik and Steffen, were too tired to go, so Stephanie stayed behind with her boys. She thought they might walk around the downtown area a little bit later to see what interesting things they could find. She thought visiting the grave might not be very exciting for two young kids.

"Marek, Uncle Milan said it might snow this afternoon so it's better that we go this morning. It will be hard to drive on the country road to the cemetery. Not only that, after we are there, we need to walk about half an hour to Great-Grandpa's site," Jana said.

"Yes, Mom. Actually, I'm glad Erik and Steffen aren't going. It would be harder for them, and hard to take care of them too. It is getting chilly," Marek remarked.

By the time they arrived at the cemetery, the cold wind had gotten stronger. They parked the car in the parking area and began to walk. Along the way they needed to rest a couple times, especially for Jana, Milan, and Martin. They were not young anymore.

Marek kept looking around trying to see if any of the area seemed familiar. But it was all different. He had never seen this place before. Then, as they drew closer, he saw the mountain on his left and a forest on his right.

"I have seen this before. It looks so familiar," Marek thought.

When they were near, Marek told his mom, "Great-grandpa's grave is on the right, not too far from those woods."

"How do you know that? You have never been here before!" Jana marveled.

"Mom, remember the dream I had? I saw this scenery in the dream. I took my mom - sorry, it was not you, it was Klara, Great-Grandma. I took her on this path to visit the grave many times after Great-Grandpa's death. Remember, in the dream I was Grandpa?" Marek explained

"Are you sure? Maybe you are dreaming now!" Jana laughed.

"Tell Uncle Milan and Uncle Martin that I can lead the way. I will show you where the grave is. We are almost there," Marek said.

Jana talked to her cousins about what Marek had said. They laughed and nodded their heads, indicating they were willing to let Marek give it a try. Within five minutes Marek, just by following his instincts, had led them to the exact grave among so many around. They were very surprised. Then Jana explained to them about the funeral scene that Marek saw in his dreams. They couldn't believe it.

Marek went directly to the spot where he had stood in his dream and closed his eyes. He could picture that he was his grandpa, Pavel, standing there for his father's funeral. His mom and sister were on his right, his brothers on his left. His two uncles and a few other people were on the other side of grave. He could feel the sadness. It felt like his dream had become reality. He had a profound feeling of loss and emptiness, but he could not explain it.

On the way back to his hotel, Marek was very quiet. Snow had started to fall. His mind was deep in thought. By the time they returned to the hotel, Stephanie and the kids had already eaten lunch and the kids were taking a nap. The rest of them went to a restaurant on the street and ordered some typical Czech food. Marek insisted the lunch was his treat, since this trip was at his request. The visit to the cemetery had fulfilled the wish that Marek had had since the very beginning of the trip. Since, in fact, he had first thought of making the trip.

Snow continued to fall during the following two days. And then Sunday, January 2, Marek's family was on their way back to Chicago. It had been a too-short visit, but it left them with many memories, especially for Marek. It seemed everything was so familiar to him when he was in the Czech Republic.

A DREAM

One month later, the memory of the trip was still on Marek's mind. On this Friday night, Marek brought his mom back to his place for the weekend. While they were sitting in the living room after dinner, he again brought up the topic of their trip.

"Mom, I am so glad that we took the trip to Czech a month ago! Everything we saw and did there is still hanging in my mind," he said.

"Me too, Marek! You know I had not seen your uncles and their families for a very long time. We should invite them to America someday. I had mentioned the possibility to them, and they were very excited," Jana said.

"Definitely! Once I can afford to buy a bigger house, we should definitely invite them here. At least, with a bigger house they wouldn't have to stay in a hotel. We could all be together as a family."

"Remember we talked about selling our stocks to buy the bigger house, Marek. When do you think we should do that?" Stephanie asked. "I've heard that people are acting a bit crazy, buying more and more stock since the market keeps rising."

"I don't know, and actually nobody knows when the best time is. The market seems to still be very favorable though. Investing in stock is just like gambling. We never know what's going to happen the next day. I believe this stock growth won't last much longer, though. We should sell our stocks by the end of the year, or at least half of them," Marek replied.

"If we change to a bigger house, I want to have a bigger kitchen and dining room. The one we have now is too small. It feels crowded even with just the three of us in it. I would also like to have more window light, I mean natural light," Stephanie said with a big smile. She had great hopes for the future.

"I could use a bigger study room," Marek said, joining in the fun of designing their dream home. "It's too small right now, and I can't keep all of my business things in there tidy. I think we also need an extra room so when your mom or my mom come to visit, they can have their own room to stay in."

Marek looked at his sons, who were busy eating but were also listening intently to their parents' conversation. Though they were still too young to understand about the stock market, they could tell their dad and mom were happy with what was happening.

"Mom! We finished. Can we go play our computer games? You said we could play Saturday," Erik asked.

"Yes, Erik. But no more than two hours," Stephanie replied.

After the boys had left the table, the adults went to the living room to continue discussing possibilities.

"The truth is, I'm frankly worried and concerned about the way the stock market has continued to rise. It's not normal. In just one year, the value of our stocks has increased more than three times. I'm afraid it's going to crash soon. Should we hang in there, or should we sell out?" Marek wondered.

"I don't know, Marek. As you said, it's a gamble, right?" Stephanie replied.

CHAPTER 5. BUSINESS TROUBLE

The last Christmas and New Year was the most profitable holiday season that Marek's company had ever experienced. The stock market just kept going up and, as people saw their investments increase, they felt free to spend money more crazily than ever. Marek hesitated to sell his stocks as he had originally planned. He thought that if he held out for just six more months, the value of his stocks would be double.

On March 11, 2000, Marek was in his office when, suddenly, there was a big disturbance among his employees.

"What's going on, Mike?" Marek stepped out of his office and asked one of the employees who was just passing by. Mike's face showed that he was worried and nervous.

"Stocks have dropped sharply on Nasdaq this morning, losing almost 500 points in three hours. Many people who invested money in stocks are very concerned about the situation. There are some arguments about whether people should sell out or buy more since stock prices have dropped so sharply," Mike said.

Almost all of the employees played the stock market in one way or another. Working morale was low. All they did was pay attention to what the stock market was doing every day. For nearly a year everyone had been so excited about the ever-rising stock market. Everyone thought they were rich.

The morning's news caught Marek's attention. He brought up the market on his computer and found that his Müller's stock also had dropped sharply, losing almost 40% of its value from just two days ago. He was seriously concerned about the situation.

"It's just a temporary drop, it will come back. It always does," Marek tried to console himself. To ease his worry about the stock market, he focused his attention on the business instead.

Two days later, his stock values had recovered by about 20%, but then a few weeks later it dropped down again, to only one-third of its original value. It was a chaotic situation for everyone. People were panicking and many companies were facing serious problems. This was a wake-up call, especially to those who had quit their jobs to spend full time playing the market.

During dinner one night, Marek was unusually quiet. Stephanie could tell that something had happed that was bothering him. He looked so solemn and had lost his smile. Even though Stephanie knew about the market crash from watching TV news broadcasts, she had not taken in how serious it was or considered how it might have affected their own investments. She had always relied on Marek's talent in business. But tonight, his worry troubled her.

"Marek? Are you okay? You seem seriously bothered by something," Stephanie asked him with concern.

"Yes, Stephanie. I'm afraid our stocks have dropped down to only 30% of their value in the last week alone. I hope it bounces back to what it used to be soon. Otherwise, we may have a big problem," Marek said with a frown.

"That means our dream about a new house is gone, right? But that's okay. We can always wait," Stephanie tried to comfort him. Even as she said it, she knew from Marek's expression that their problem was more serious than the loss of a possible new home.

"I worry that if our company's stocks continue to drop, we might be facing bankruptcy," Marek told her.

After that, dinner was very quiet as Marek's mind was somewhere else.

An Unfortunate Disaster

Each day the situation continued to get worse. One September 11, 2001, the attacks on New York's World Trade Center accelerated the stock market drop. The whole world was shocked and expressed sorrow for the more than 2,500 people who were killed. The New York Stock Exchange was forced to suspend trading for four sessions. At Marek's company, his employees' mood reached the lowest point yet. Everyone who invested money in stocks had lost their ability to smile.

One night, three weeks before Christmas of 2001, Marek received a frantic telephone call around 2 in the morning. Mr. Brown, the landlord of the warehouse where Marek's business stored its goods, was on the line.

"Mr. Muller, I need to tell you some very bad news! It was a disaster, a terrible disaster!" Mr. Brown exclaimed.

"What has happened, Mr. Brown?" Marek asked through a drowsy haze. He had been deeply asleep and was still trying to wake up.

"The fire! The warehouse building was on fire two hours ago and almost everything in the entire building was destroyed," Mr. Brown said.

Müller's Import & Export shared warehouse space with three other companies. The warehouse owned by Mr. Brown was a two-story building. Marek's company and the others shared the ground floor with two big rooms.

"How did it happen?" Marek asked with concern. His company had just received delivery of some big orders from China, Vietnam, and India. All of these goods were to be sold during the Christmas season. Usually, the profits the company made during the holidays accounted for nearly one-half of the entire year's profit. If all of the goods in storage at the warehouse had been destroyed, it would seriously compromise his business, especially right before Christmas.

Marek woke up completely at this shocking news. Stephanie had also woken up when the telephone rang and had been listening to the conversation. She paid attention carefully.

"How much of the first floor survived?" Marek asked.

"The Fire Marshall doesn't know what happened. All he knows is that the fire started on the second floor and spread to the ground floor. I am very sorry, Mr. Müller. I was just there. I believe everything is gone. What was not burned will be damaged by water," Mr. Brown said.

"Mr. Brown, this is a huge disaster for me! My goods for the Christmas season only just arrived a couple of days ago. I hadn't managed to purchase insurance for these goods yet since they just arrived. Do you have fire insurance for your building, Mr. Brown?" Marek asked.

"Yes, I do. But the maximum the insurance company will cover for goods is two million dollars. I don't think two million dollars will cover all of the lost goods of four companies," Mr. Brown replied.

"Mr. Brown, we can't do anything about this right now. I'll come see you in the morning and we can discuss this matter." Marek hung up the phone sadly.

Stephanie looked at Marek with great concern. He gathered her into his arms and held on tight.

"Oh, Stephanie! This is the worst time to have this kind of disaster! Timing is so important to us, and now it's only three weeks before Christmas." Marek couldn't help the tears that escaped from of his eyes and rolled down his face.

Stephanie didn't know how to console him. All she could do was hold on to him in return and try to comfort him.

"Try to sleep, Stephanie. I need to be alone for a while," Marek said. "I'll be in the living room." He got up and left the bedroom.

Marek felt his stomach roil. It felt like he had to throw up. He had been experiencing stomach pain for nearly eight months now, ever since the stock market problems had begun. He went to the kitchen and found some Pepto-Bismol.

"I think I may have an ulcer," he thought as he tipped a cup of medicine into his mouth.

"What could I possibly do to save this crisis?" he pondered deeply.

Marek went to his study and sat on the meditation cushion. Usually this corner would bring him some peace and calmness. But tonight, his worries were too much to bear. He could not calm down. He could not help that his tears flowed freely. He needed to cry it out, to release all of the pressure that had accumulated in his mind and body. After ten minutes or so, he felt calmer.

"What has happened, has happened! I cannot do anything to change that. At least, I still have a wonderful wife and two beautiful children," he tried to comfort himself. After the shock, he was facing the cruel truth.

Two mornings later when the TV news reported on the fire, the stock value of Müller's Import & Export, Inc. fell down to only 10% of what it had been 18 months ago. His company now faced the possibility of having to declare bankruptcy. Marek knew that his company would need at least seven million dollars to save it. This was a huge amount for such a small company.

Actually, according to the news, there were already many small- or medium-sized companies filing bankruptcy due to the stock crash.

"Will Müller's Import & Export be the next one? I should have sold my stocks a year ago," Marek thought, his mind filled with deep regret.

That was the worst Christmas they had ever experienced. Though Marek tried his best to hide his worry in front of his mom, wife, and kids, they all knew what was happening. But if their holiday was not as cheerful as usual, at least it was peaceful.

On December 27, the fire investigator from the insurance company concluded the fire had been started by a faulty transformer on the second floor of the warehouse.

"Hi, Mr. Müller, I have some good news for you," Mr. Brown said in a phone call to Marek's office. "After their investigation my insurance company has decided to cover the loss. According to their calculations, your portion of the payout will be roughly $350,000. I'm sorry that it's not more, but this is what they will cover."

Marek was alone in his office with his secretary, Margaret, when the call came in. Everyone else had decided to take a long vacation from Christmas Eve to New Year's. Actually, after the fire, there wasn't much work to do at the company anyway.

"Thank you for the news, Mr. Brown. I think it will ease my financial situation a little bit," Marek said.

Marek did have his own fire insurance that protected the older goods that had been inside the warehouse. But since he had not had time to insure the new goods that arrived just before the fire, those goods were a total loss. If his insurance company agreed to pay on the old storage goods, he might receive $150,000 or so. Most damaging of all, however, was that the business had missed out on the top Christmas selling season.

Remembering that he would receive at least some money from the insurance companies somehow made him feel a little bit at ease and less nervous. He felt lighter today. After he went home, he told Stephanie about the fire compensation. Both of them knew this compensation would extend the company's life, but to save it, a miracle would need to happen. In order to survive, he might have to lay off some non-crucial employees.

CHAPTER 6. SEEKING HELP

Though the warm and sunny weather in March 2002 was nicer than normal in Chicago, Marek's heart was dark and grey. His savings in the bank, along with the insurance payout, would be just enough to get his company through another ten months of payroll – if he did not invest any money in purchasing more goods. Without some outside financial support, he would have to declare bankruptcy. That was not what he wanted. His health and weight were rapidly deteriorating due to the ceaseless worry. When he happened to see himself in a mirror, he could not believe how bad he looked. In just a little more than 18 months he felt he had aged at least ten years.

Marek walked out of the bank feeling deeply depressed and sad. This was the third bank that had rejected his application for an emergency loan because he did not have any convincing collateral. Furthermore, almost all of the banks were being very cautious about giving loans of any kind during this stock crisis. Marek knew that even if he sold the company building that he owned, it would not be enough to pay off the debt the company owed so far. He also knew that his two uncles were not rich enough to help, even if they tried. He began to pin some slim hopes on purchasing lottery tickets, even though he knew the chance of winning was nearly zero.

Marek was on the edge of collapse. He had lost nearly 20 pounds and his stomach problem continued to bother him. He had forgotten how to smile. He began to pray to God, Buddha, or any holy divinity to help him. Though his prayers brought him some hope, deep down he also felt that those divinities, if they existed, would not pay attention to him.

He tried to meditate, hoping that the meditation would help him relax and find peace and calmness. Meditation had always brought him peace and calmness before, but he also knew that meditation could offer him only a temporary escape from facing the truthful and harsh world. However, his current attempts to meditate were not going well. Whenever he calmed down, his problems would emerge again and affect his meditation. He could never manage to enter the same level of meditation that he used to.

"I must stand up strong. I cannot fall and I will not. I have a family and I am still young," he kept reminding himself.

Marek was beyond tired and desperately needed a nice rest, both physically and mentally. Stephanie and his mom understood the situation but couldn't offer much help. All they could do was hold him to try to comfort him.

"It wouldn't be a good selling season anyway due to this stock crisis. People don't have any money to spend. Anyway, the insurance money will make it possible for me to pay my employees' salaries until January of next year. We will be able to survive," he tried to reassure himself.

On Sunday morning, he woke up late and went to his study. His mind was calmer and more peaceful today. He had just sat down on his meditation cushion when suddenly the phone rang.

"Hi, Marek! How are you doing? I hope you are well," his friend Steve said.

"Not too good, I'm afraid, Steve. My company is facing the possibility of bankruptcy. The stock market crashed, you know, and in addition, the warehouse my goods were stored in had a fire three weeks before last Christmas. I lost everything, and the goods weren't insured."

"What did you say? You lost all your goods in a fire last year? I'm very sorry to hear that. I didn't know. Marek, I wish I could offer you some financial help!" Steve said.

"The worst of it is that the value of my company's stocks has fallen to only 10% compared with the beginning of last year. Steve! I am in deep trouble," Marek sighed.

"I know, Marek. I also lost almost all of my savings. I was very sad for a while. Later, I woke up and faced the situation. After all, it's only money, and money comes and goes. I still have my health. I still fortunately have enough money to survive. It's not the end of the world. Although these last several months have taught me the lesson that I shouldn't take the risk of trusting in stock investments. Again, I'm so sorry that I can't help you financially."

"I know you would if you were able, pal. Well, I wish I had gone to that seminar with you last summer! I still have a lot of questions. Since the stock market crashed and the warehouse burned, I haven't been able to calm down enough to meditate even once."

"I believe that if you can't meditate, it's because of the environment around you. If you wish to calm down and make your mind clear, you will need to get out of Chicago for a while," Steve counseled him.

"I can't Steve! I have so many burdens and responsibilities resting on my shoulders right now. I can't just leave!"

"Well! Then tell me, have you been able to improve your situation in your current state? Will you be able to solve your problems? If not, it will be even more harmful to your health to not make a change. Remember, once you get sick, your hopes will be even slimmer. The Chinese have a saying, 'know how to pick up and know how to drop it.' Can you drop it for a while?" Steve said in an attempt to help Marek.

"Actually, I've lost at least 20 pounds and my stomach has been giving me trouble for many months already. I am utterly exhausted both mentally and physically. Steve, this seems to be my destiny!" Marek said sadly.

"Why don't you go to see Master Tang and stay at his retreat center for a while. You'll see how great a place it is for your meditation practice and spiritual cultivation. Furthermore, if you have questions, Master Tang is right there for you to ask him."

"I don't know... I do need to calm down so I can solve this crisis... Thank you, Steve. I may just do it."

Marek talked to his wife and Stephanie agreed that he needed to find a way to keep his mind peaceful and calm. She had been very worried about his health.

"I'm sorry, Stephanie. If I leave you alone with the kids for two weeks, are you sure you'll be okay?"

"Marek, it won't be a problem! I'm sure I can handle it. You need to arrange for someone to take care of the company while you are gone, though."

"I know. I'm actually confident that Margaret will be able to handle the company for two weeks since this is not a busy season. Usually, March and April are when I make my first buying trips to those countries from which we import our goods. Since we don't have any money for buying goods right now, business is slow and not busy at all."

"Well, in that case, just go and don't worry about us. I just want you to be able to find some peace and calmness on the mountain."

That afternoon, when Marek was in his office, he dialed the number for Master Tang that Steve had given to him.

"Hello, this is Master Tang speaking. How can I help you?"

"Master Tang, my name is Marek. I'm a friend of Steve Zhang. I wonder if I can come to visit the center and practice with you for two weeks?"

"Oh! You are Marek. Steve has talked about you several times when he's been here. Of course, you are welcome to come and stay with us. Once you have your flight itinerary, please let me know so I can send someone to pick you up at the airport. Remember, you must fly to Eureka/Arcata airport. That is about 280 miles north of San Francisco."

"Yes, Steve has already explained that to me. It will be an honor to meet you. I am thinking of coming next Monday. Once I have my flight itinerary, I'll send the information to you by e-mail."

"Okay! I will be waiting for your further contact. It will be so nice to meet you as well. Bye now," Master Tang replied and hung up.

Now that he had permission from Master Tang, Marek immediately purchased a ticket from Chicago to Eureka/Arcata airport. Once he received confirmation of his reservation, he sent the information to Master Tang.

ADVICE

The following Monday Master Tang's student, Colin, went to the Eureka/Arcata airport to pick Marek up. Since Colin didn't know Marek and wouldn't recognize him, he held a sign with the name of the retreat center in his hands. Once Marek's airplane had arrived, as he entered the arrivals hall, Marek recognized the sign and walked over to where Colin was standing.

"Hi, I'm Marek. You must be from the retreat center to pick me up."

"Yes, hi. I'm Colin. Nice to meet you! Do you have any luggage that you checked in?"

"No. All I have is this carry-on! I'll only be staying two weeks. Do you know Steve Zhang, my good friend?" Marek asked.

"Of course! He is everyone's favorite. He's a nice guy and gets along with everybody. Let's go then. It's a 90-minute drive to the center. If you're tired, you can take a nap in the car."

"I'm okay. I like the feel of northern California. I've never been here before."

After they passed through Arcata and Eureka and gradually entered Fortuna, Marek could see a wide field with many cattle grazing in it. On either side of Freeway 101, he noticed beautiful hills and mountains. Directly alongside the freeway ran the crystal-clear water

of the Eel River. The air was fresh, and the overall feeling of the coun-
tryside was fantastic. This was not the same feeling that he had in big
cities like Chicago.

The surroundings offered him a natural and peaceful calm feeling.
After driving 40 minutes or so, the car entered the redwood forest
area. These 300-foot-tall redwoods created an energy within their
surroundings that made itself felt inside a person's inner being. Gradually, Marek's mental tension eased. After a few deep breaths of the
wonderfully pure air, he felt himself relax. It seemed that his worries
about his business were already receding behind him.

"Steve was right. I needed to get out of Chicago. I need to find the
peace and calmness deep in my heart again. I need to find myself and
regain my confidence and strength," Marek reminded himself.

Finally, the car reached the town of Miranda and turned off onto a
side road. After ten minutes or so, it merged onto a private stone drive.

"We're almost there," Colin said.

"How big is the center?"

"Well, it covers 243 acres of land! But most of the activities are
held on the top of the mountain where the view and the energy are
best," Colin replied.

At last the car reached the top of the mountain. Marek could see a
greenhouse with a good-sized organic garden on the right-hand side
of the driveway. Directly in front of the car was a big, round building.
Next to this main building grew a beautiful, tall madrone tree. Marek
later found out the tree was at least 300 years old. Under the tree, there
was an octagonal gazebo. And when you stood in front of the round
building, the view as you looked out over a valley to the opposite
mountain was fantastic!

Just before the car arrived at the parking lot, Colin pointed his finger at a mountain peak. "See that peak? It's called Bear Butte. It was
an old volcano. According to native people, it erupted about 800 years
ago. Even though it isn't active now, the energy that emerges from it
continues to feed this valley. That's why the energy is so strong here."

"Wow! It is so beautiful and peaceful here. Do you get your electricity and water supply from the city?"

"No! You must be kidding. There are no cities here. There's only the town with a population of 350. We get our electricity mainly from solar panels with a propane generator as back up. Our water comes from a well and spring and is perfectly pure. The best things about this place, other than its strong Qi field, are the water and fresh air. It's rare to find such a place in the world."

They had arrived just in time for dinner. Colin brought Marek into the round building where there were a few guest rooms on the upper floor and got him settled in a suite. Then, Colin took him back down to the dining area on the lower level and introduced him, "Master Tang, here is Mr. Marek Müller."

"Nice to meet you, Marek. Steve talked about you a few times when he was here. Welcome!"

"It's great to meet you, sir." Marek bowed to Master Tang.

"First, eat dinner and then rest today. You must be tired from traveling. Now that you are here, please release your mind from city life, just relax and be calm. If you meditate a few days, you will feel the strength of Qi in this area."

"Why is the Qi field so different in this place?" Marek asked curiously.

"Well, you see, there is a creek on the north of this land, facing north with water, so it is the Yin Pole of this land. Here, where we are, as you see, we face the south and there is a mountain in front of us. It is the Yang Pole. This land is formalized with two Yin-Yang poles. So, the Qi can be stored to an abundant level. As a matter of fact, if you look around this land, you will see this place is surrounded by higher mountains in a circle while this place is situated at the center. The best part is that old Bear Butte Volcano. The Qi from the volcano continues to release and influence the Qi field in the valley."

"Yes! Colin told me about that volcano already."

"You cannot feel much now since you just arrived and are excited or tired. You must allow yourself to calm down first. After a few days, you will feel it through meditation," Master Tang explained. "Now, go eat and rest. Remember, the meditation session begins at 6 in the morning here," Master Tang continued.

After dinner and a shower, Marek called his wife on his cell phone.

"Hi Stephanie, it's me. I just arrived a couple hours ago. It's very beautiful here. The best part is, since it's so remote from the city, this space brings my mind peace and calm. I wish you were here with me," he told her.

"I'm glad you arrived safely, Marek. I'm not going to contact you unless I have something urgent to tell you. All I want for you to do is relax and find yourself again, especially your confidence."

"Thank you, Stephanie. I'm so glad that I have a wife like you, so understanding and supportive. I am going to rest now. It's been a long time since I've had a peaceful mind. Good night!"

Marek readied himself for bed and lay down. He tossed around for a while but couldn't sleep. Once his body had calmed down, his monkey mind started churning out thoughts full of excitement mixed with expectation. And, of course, his worries about his business also came back to bother him. He thought of his past, present, and future.

"I have to do what Steve said and stop all these thoughts, at least for these two weeks. I remember what the Embryonic Breathing book said, that deep, soft, and slender breathing is the key to calming down your mind and bringing you to a deep relaxed state," Marek reminded himself.

He kept trying. Unfortunately, the more he tried, the worse it was.

"I must downplay the activities of my conscious mind. I should bring my Qi down to my guts, the Real Lower Dan Tian, the Qi battery." Again, he reminded himself.

He inhaled deeply and used his mind to lead the Qi down from his head to his abdominal area while at the same time allowing this conscious mind to fade out. When the Qi reached his guts, he simply relaxed and allowed his breath to go out naturally. After twenty minutes or so, he finally fell asleep.

Marek slept until 4 in the morning without once waking up. It would be 6 a.m. in Chicago - the time he usually woke up to meditate. But at the retreat center in California, it was very quiet and still dark outside. After six hours of deep sleep, he felt completely rested. He sat up and put his pillow against the headboard. He meditated and tried to bring his mind to a semi-sleeping state. In twenty minutes or so, he entered the deep state. This was the first time in the last eighteen months that he was able to enter this semi-sleeping state. He was able to maintain his mind in emptiness for a while.

When he roused from his meditation, it was already 5:45 a.m. That was one of the longest meditations he had ever had. He was very surprised.

"Now I understand why I have to drop out of the human matrix to be able to calm down. These two weeks will be precious time for me," he thought.

Marek went downstairs to the lecture hall where the group meditation would take place. Master Tang was already there, fixing some herbal tea for everyone.

"You can find a meditation cushion and pillow for yourself in that corner to set up your meditation place. We face the east so that we can absorb the energy of the early sun," Master Tang told him.

After Marek set up his place, he went to greet the others. There were eight people in the room in total. Some of the students present would be on the mountain for training for a few years. Some, just like him, had come from various places and countries to have a short visit.

By 6 a.m., everyone was in position. A weak audio gong sounded from a stereo. The sound felt like it had been generated from deep inside a mountain, like a calling to lead everyone to a profound meditative state. Once Marek paid attention to the sound, he felt it resonating with his limbic system, with the very center of his head.

In just ten minutes, Marek was able to enter the semi-sleeping meditative state. Subconsciously, he could also feel the Qi generated by the others. It was amazing! That feeling that he was exchanging Qi with others! By coordinating his breathing with the sound of the gong, he was able to match the others' breathing. Soon, the Qi built up by the group had reached a high level that Marek had never experienced before.

"That was why the gong was played during group meditation in monasteries," he thought, and then dismissed the thought. He needed to downplay his conscious mind again; otherwise, he would regain complete consciousness and lose the subconscious feeling.

After 45 minutes of meditation, the gong sound ended and was replaced by soft music. Everyone resumed his or her normal state and followed a routine of recovery that involved stretching the torso and arms, moving the spine in a wave, massaging the knees, and stimulating the soles of the feet, among other things.

Marek felt so peaceful. He could begin to comprehend the monks' peaceful life.

"If I were not married and did not have children, I would stay here for the rest of my life. This place has offered me a calm and peaceful feeling that I could never have received from the outside world," he thought.

When he had first arrived, Marek had had tons of questions that he immediately wanted to ask Master Tang. Now, from his peaceful mind, he knew he was not ready yet. He needed to wait and search for his deeper feeling first.

In addition to the meditation practice, while he was at the retreat center Marek also joined the others for their Taijiquan and Qigong practice. He ate healthy foods, breathed the fresh air, slept well, and sometimes climbed mountains. He also read some of the Qigong and Taijiquan books in the center's library. Gradually, the mental burdens and pressures that had built up on him began to ease significantly. He felt he was regaining a bit more of his health every day.

After one week, though he had not yet recovered his physical health, Marek's mental status was much more stable. He could see things calmly and clearly instead of panicking and worrying. In addition, through the group discussions and Q&A sessions on Tuesday and Thursday afternoons, he was able to reaffirm the accuracy of what he had learned from Steve and from reading his book. His mind was much clearer about the whole concept of Embryonic Breathing.

At the beginning of the second week, Marek believed that he was ready to ask some of his deep questions that he had not yet heard discussed among the group. During break one afternoon, he saw Master Tang sitting on a chair next to the gazebo and decided to go ask him some questions.

AN UNFORGETTABLE LESSON

"Master Tang, I'm sorry to bother you. But is it possible for me to ask you some questions? It's very important to me," Marek asked as he approached Master Tang.

"Certainly, Marek. Actually, when you had just arrived last week, I saw from your face that something had been bothering you for quite some time. It made me feel that there was a shadow following you. However, after one week, I can also see that you are untying the knots tangled in your mind. I hope I can help you untie them faster. First, tell me the problem you have."

Marek was very surprised that Master Tang had noticed that he was troubled. He briefly explained to Master Tang what had happened to his business and how Steve had tried to help him calm down his mind through meditation. Finally, he told Master Tang about the dream he had had and the scene that appeared in his meditation.

Master Tang listened patiently to his story, then said, "Marek, you should know one important fact: where there is a consequence, there must be a cause. Everything that happens has its reason. You may not see the reason right away; however, after time passes, it will become clear. What happened to you may have a reason behind it."

"But I have never harmed anyone or taken advantage of others!" Marek protested. "Why and how could this happen to me? Why would God or Buddha punish me for a harm I have never committed? I have always been questioning about 'what is the meaning of my life' since I was a child. But now, with my business troubles, I am even more anxious to know it." He looked at Master Tang with eagerness, hoping to finally hear the answers he sought.

"Marek. You already know about the concept of two poles, Yin and Yang, from Steve and last week's discussion. You must have also acknowledged that there are two worlds, dimensions, or spaces coexisting in nature. Chinese call them 'Yin Jian' (Yin Space) and 'Yang Jian' (Yang Space). The Yin Space is the spiritual world while the Yang Space is the material world. According to the *Dao De Jing*, the Dao is the spiritual world, and the De is the material world. De, or the material world, is the manifestation of the Dao, the spiritual world. Though there are two spaces, however, in function, it is only one, since both spaces influence and correspond with each other simultaneously. Since we were created and developed in these two worlds together, we also have two lives in our body, physical life and spiritual life. Tell me, Marek. When you talk about the meaning of life, which life are you talking about?"

Marek thought about this for a while, then answered, "I believe that if I want to understand my life, I need to know both. Steve tried to explain the Yin-Yang worlds concept to me and their relationship, but I'm still not quite clear on the deep aspect of its meaning. Judging by scientific research to date, even though we have come to understand many things about our material world, we still don't have much of an idea about the spiritual world."

"You are correct, Marek. That was why all religions were generated in the past and tried to interpret the spirit. Unfortunately, this intention has triggered spiritual abuse and domination. Since then, our spiritual development has been restricted by religious dogma. From this dogma and brainwashing, we conquered and killed each other.

Actually, you know, once the religions got involved in political power, glory, dignity, and wealth, the spiritual understanding and development had already become shallow."

Master Tang looked at Marek and saw his reaction, "The reason that you are confused about the meaning of life is because you don't have a clear understanding of your spiritual life. If your concern is only the meaning of your physical life, then you would never comprehend the whole picture of the meaning of life since you have missed half of it. In order to comprehend the meaning of life, you must know and feel both material and spiritual sides."

"But, Master Tang, how can we access our spirit? We cannot see it, even though we can feel it's existence."

"Marek! You just said the key word to accessing the spiritual world. Remember, you may see the material world, but for the spiritual world you must develop your feeling. The deeper and more profound you are able to feel, the more you can comprehend it. From past experience, it is understood that in order to reach the deep feeling of spiritual world, you must practice meditation. This practice is just learning a language; the more you practice the more you understand it. What I mean is, through correct meditation, you will be able to access the spiritual world. Once you are able to enter it, you will feel there is a huge beautiful garden that has never been explored by most people."

"But Master Tang, aren't there many different kinds of meditation? Is any one type of meditation better than the others for spiritual development?" Marek asked.

"Naturally, there are so many kinds of meditation developed by different cultures in the past. Almost all of them were searching for the meaning of the spiritual world. However, through thousands year of practice and experience, some were able to reach a deep level of understanding and most others remained shallow."

"Is that why you teach us the Embryonic Breathing method? Is it the best and most effective way to reach the Yin world?" Marek asked.

"Yes. You know, as we explained last week, the conscious mind is more related to the material world while the subconscious mind is more connected to the spiritual world. Embryonic Breathing Meditation is the key to reaching the spiritual world."

"Master Tang! Are you implying that if I want to understand my trouble, I need to access the Yin world, otherwise, I will not be able to see the entire picture of the problem?"

Master Tang nodded his head with a smile.

Marek continued, "I understand that in order to reach the spiritual world, I must cultivate my subconscious mind. The subconscious mind is the key to the entrance to the spiritual world. Am I right, Master Tang?"

"Yes. Since our conscious mind plays trick and has a mask, it is not truthful. Nature is truthful. Only truthful feeling is able to access it. That is why you have to downplay your conscious mind and allow your subconscious mind to wake up and grow. When this happens, the mask on your face will drop off. This is the first step of spiritual cultivation, called 'Self-Recognition.'"

"I remember Steve telling me about this. The next stage of cultivation is 'Self-Awareness.' Is that right?" Marek asked excitedly. He felt he was finally starting to understand.

"Yes, from removal of the mask, you will be truthful and see yourself clearly internally. With this recognition, you will be able to build a higher level of awareness in both the material and spiritual worlds. When this happens, you will see how both worlds influence and correspond with each other. For example, any spiritual energy imbalance in the Yin World eventually will be bounced back or manifested in the Yang World. Naturally, in the same token, any deed or action you have conducted and committed in the Yang world will also influence the balance of the Yin World. This is called Bao Ying in Chinese and means retribution. It is called 'karma' in India."

"Does that mean the business trouble happening to me right now might be caused from a Yin imbalance?"

"I believe so."

"Then, how can the imbalance have happened? I didn't do anything bad in the past!"

"Let me explain to you more clearly if I may, Marek. However, we should first be clear on an important thing. Now, please answer my question. When you see objects around you, what do your eyes see? Do they see matter or just sense energy emitted from matter?" Master Tang asked.

"Of course, what we see is matter," Marek answered without thinking. Then, just a moment later, "Wait a minute! Actually, all our eyes see is the different wavelengths emitted from the objects. We don't see matter." Marek had never really thought of this in the past.

"That's right. What you see in matter with different shapes and colors actually are different frequencies released from matter. Let me ask you another question, Marek. When you see a person, how much matter do you actually see? I mean percentage?"

This question confused Marek at first. After he thought about it, he answered carefully, "I don't know. Actually, what I see is the energy emitted from the body."

"Okay! Now you see, your body is constructed by cells, cells are constructed by molecules, and then, the molecules are constructed by atoms. Right? As we know, our body contains 96% of hydrogen, oxygen, nitrogen, and carbon and 4% of other minerals. If you take a closer look at an atom, for example, the hydrogen atom structure, you will see it is constructed by a nucleus and an electron. If you magnified this atom a million times, you will see the size of the nucleus is just like a football, the electron will be a size of a baseball orbiting the nucleus. The radius of the electron's orbit is about one mile. All the remaining space is empty. That means the matter in an atom is actually very tiny and ignorable. Usually, the atom will stay at ground state only under absolute zero temperature. That is minus 459.67 degrees Fahrenheit or minus 273.15 degrees Celsius."

"But there is no such low temperature around us," Marek said.

"That is right! When we see matter, all atoms are in excited energy state. What you see of the objects is the energy released from the excited vibrating atoms."

"Wow! That means actually what we see when we look at each other is only the energy vibration instead of matter itself."

"That is correct. When different atoms construct a molecule, the molecule has its vibration. When different molecules construct a cell, a cell has its vibration. As you know, different cells with different DNA construct each one of us. That means each one of our body's energy vibration is unique. Naturally, different parts of the organs for different people will also vibrate differently. For example, the vibration of your limbic system can also be very different from others, and this vibration frequency is decided by your genes or DNA. You know, if there is another person who has the same or similar vibration frequency, the cells in your limbic system will synchronize with each other."

"A-hah! Is that why many sets of twins are able to communicate with each other, even when they are far apart?" Marek asked.

"Yes. This limbic system's vibration frequency band is unique for different genes. The most important part of this vibration frequency band, it does not matter which person or what animals, are included in the frequency bandwidth of nature. That is why almost all animals can feel the natural energy change and also are able to access their genetic memory. That is why in Embryonic Breathing Meditation, you would like to minimize your conscious mind, so you are able to build a higher sensitivity of your subconscious mind in your limbic system. That means to widen your limbic system's vibration band and improve the sensitivity of connection to the spiritual world."

"Does that mean the scene I saw in my dream might be caused by this spiritual vibration synchronization, Master Tang?"

"Very likely." Master Tang looked at Marek with a smile.

"But that would mean I was synchronizing with my grandpa who died nearly fifty years ago. I don't understand how that can happen."

"Well, Marek, to understand this, first you must acknowledge that every action we have done and the thoughts we have created in the past have been recorded in nature."

Marek was again confused. "How can a deed or a thought be recorded in nature?" Marek looked at Master Tang in bewilderment.

"My dear Marek! You know all material degenerates with time and is affected by the energy vibration around it. What I meant is the molecular structure of all material is changed constantly with time. Any vibration around it will also influence the degeneration process and be recorded in the matter. For example, when we talk, the degeneration process of objects around us will be affected by the frequencies of our conversation and recorded. One day, science may have the technology to trace the recorded information that had happened in the past around the objects."

"Amazing! I would never have considered that. But how about a thought, though? How can a thought be recorded?"

"You see, thought is generated from conscious mind in the brain. Different thoughts have different vibrational frequencies. You know the mind that is related to the spirit is connected with the spiritual dimension or world. When a thought is generated, this vibration will influence the energy field of the spiritual side and be recorded. That means if you have an evil thought, it will be recorded. Naturally, if you have a good thought, it will also be recorded. When time passes, the energy difference will be built up. When this energy has reached to a certain level, it will manifest into the Yang, or material world, so the energy in spiritual world can regain its balance. This is the cause of karma."

"Does this mean my grandpa's thoughts in the past generated an imbalance that needed to be manifested in the material world?"

"Yes. His thoughts were recorded in the spiritual world. Now, it has bounced back to you since you have his genes and a similar vibrational frequency."

"How come this kind of dream has never appeared to my sister?"

"Well! If your sister pays too much attention to her conscious mind and neglects her subconscious feelings, she will not sense it. Usually, this kind of subconscious sensitivity is developed through meditation. Some people were able to build this connection through dreams, like you. You know, sleeping is a state of deep meditation, only the conscious mind is not there."

"I am so happy to know all of this. It has unlocked the answers to many of my questions and confusions. But, please, Master Tang. Please tell me how I can develop my subconscious mind to a point where I can reach the thoughts that my grandpa recorded?"

"Once you have reached the semi-sleeping state during meditation, you have to use your conscious mind to tune your subconscious vibrational frequency to the event till it is clear. Naturally, your conscious mind cannot be too strong and dominates the thinking. If this happens, you will lose contact. You must be patient and keep searching for the right frequency just like you are tuning the radio for a specific station. Once you know how to contact it, it will become easier each time. This kind of spiritual communication is called *Shen Tong* in Chinese Qigong practice."

"Will I be able to reach other information that is not close to my genetic vibration?"

"Yes, if you have reached a high level. You will be able to widen your synchronization frequency bandwidth and receive other information. That is why it is said in Chinese Qigong society that once you have reached to a certain level of meditation, you will not need a teacher from the physical world since you are able to find unlimited information in the spiritual world."

"How can I reach this level, Master Tang?"

"There are two different levels of spiritual communications. One is when you build up a high level of spiritual energy sensitivity in your limbic system; you are able to feel and sense a corresponding frequency and communicate with it. That is what you have experienced in your dream or meditation. However, in order to widen your frequency bandwidth to acquire more information, you need to re-open your Third Eye. The Third Eye is called the 'Heaven Eye' in Chinese Qigong since you are able to communicate with the natural energy or spirit freely. Heaven here means nature in Chinese society. Once you have opened the Third Eye, you will suddenly be able to sense natural energy changes or disturbances and predict future phenomena. When you have reached this level, you will also have the capability of telepathy and become a prophet."

"Is that what is called Buddhahood in Buddhism and Immortality in Daoism?"

"No. It is only a stage of spiritual enlightenment since your spirit is able to unite with the natural spirit. In order to reach Buddhahood or immortality, you need to grow your spirit until it can survive without re-entering reincarnation. As we know in the past, when a person dies, his spiritual body and physical body will be separated. The physical body re-enters the natural recycling process while the spiritual body will re-enter the spiritual world and wait for the opportunity to be re-born. If this spirit cannot find a suitable new residence and be re-born in certain period of time, the energy of this spirit will dissipate into nature and be gone forever. However, if you know how to absorb the natural spiritual energy to nourish your spirit without relying on the physical body, your spirit can live forever. This is the concept of spiritual eternity and means Buddhahood or immortality."

Since it was getting late, and the afternoon session of lessons would begin in a few minutes, it was time to end the conversation.

"Thank you very much, Master Tang. This talk has helped me more than you know. It has solved many questions that have been running through my mind during the last ten years," Marek said.

Marek continued to thoughtfully ponder the conversation he had with Master Tang. By the end of the second week, he had reached a greater depth of calmness and peace than he had known in the last couple of years. With new guidelines and understanding, he was more confident than ever. He began to comprehend how the Yin and Yang

Worlds corresponded and influenced each other. He also understood the possible reasons for what had happened to him over the last couple years. He began to understand that his problem was caused by an imbalance between the Yin and Yang worlds. Nature had been trying to regain its balance during the last couple years. He felt like the circumstances of his life were just fulfilling a destiny that had already been arranged for him. He deeply knew this period of rebalancing was not yet at an end and, perhaps, was only at the beginning of manifesting. He did not know what the result would be, but he was pretty confident now that he would pass this crisis. Now, he knew what he needed to do.

By the time Marek had to leave the retreat center, other than regaining a calm and peaceful mind, he had also re-established the most important thing, his confidence. He was no longer scared or worried about what the future would hold.

When he went to say good-bye to Master Tang, he spoke sincerely from his heart, "Master! I am so deeply grateful to you for what you have taught me. I'm now ready to face the new challenges in front of me. I hope to see you again."

"Marek! When I saw the shadow on your face was fading out, I knew you were on the right path. I just wish you the best."

RETURNING TO CHICAGO

When Marek returned to Chicago, Stephanie couldn't believe how much he had changed in just two weeks. She was so happy for him. She could see that Marek's confidence had returned. Now, other than his morning's meditation, Marek also added another session right before he went to bed. Each time he reached a deep semi-sleeping state, he tried to use his conscious mind to search for the correct frequency to connect with his grandpa's recording.

Then, during one morning's meditation, the scene of the funeral suddenly appeared again. He looked at his mom standing on his right.

The sorrow he felt grew deeper and deeper. Abruptly, another scene appeared in the meditation. Now he was facing a beautiful woman.

"Darina, today is your 32nd birthday! Thank you for giving me the very happy last five years."

"Pavel! I am very happy to be married to you. I just wish our first child, Marek, were still alive. I am very sorry."

"We will have another one, Darina. We are still young," Pavel comforted her.

He paused for a while in thought, then spoke again.

"Darina! I want to tell you that I opened a Swiss bank account last week. I worry that the situation here is not stable and will get worse. I want you to remember the secret code to access our account in Switzerland." He wrote it down on a piece of paper and gave it to her. "I have also written down the codes in my diary. Just in case I also forget," Pavel said.

"Oh Pavel, I will never remember it! It has too many numbers," Darina said with a smile.

After that, the scene began to blur. Only a few words kept ringing in Marek's mind, "secret code" and "diary." He roused from his meditation and was surprised to discover that he had been sitting for nearly an hour. It felt like it had only been a few minutes!

"Pavel was my grandpa's name and Darina was my grandma's. Judging by their conversation, it was taking place after the time my first uncle, Marek, died and before my mom was born. It must have been around 1928. Five years after my grandpa's marriage," Marek thought.

In his subconscious mind, the words "secret code, diary" kept repeating themselves. Marek's curiosity took him to the living room where he looked at his grandpa's family photo again, the copy of his mom's original that he had had framed a year ago. His tears flowed down his face without thought when he saw his grandpa's face in the photo, and his heart was filled with emotion.

Throughout the following week, the funeral and the conversation scenes reappeared frequently during his meditation. It felt like his grandpa's spirit was trying to remind him of something.

"Did Grandpa have a diary? Is the secret bank code he was talking about written down? My mom has never mentioned anything about a written secret code or diary."

He decided to talk to his mom that Sunday.

CHAPTER 7. A HOPE

It was only 7:30 in the morning when Marek went to see his mom. Stephanie and his two boys were still sleeping. This was Sunday, and they would not wake up until 8:30 or so. Marek had tossed and turned the whole night last night. There were so many questions in his mind that he needed to know the answers to. He knew that his mom always woke up early, usually around 6:30. When he arrived, he used his key to open the door. He didn't want to ring the bell since he didn't want to wake up Susan. He had a key to his sister's home since he came to see his mom so often.

When he went in, he found his mom in the kitchen.

"I thought I heard a car pulling into the driveway," Jana said. "It was you, Marek. Why are you here so early?"

"Mom! Did Grandpa write a diary?" Marek asked anxiously.

"I have no idea. Usually it was kept secret. Wait! My mom mentioned that after my father's death, she read something that my father left behind and she was crying over it for a few weeks," Jana replied. She paused for a moment. "Yes! I remember she mentioned she was looking for some code in a diary, but she couldn't find it."

"Is it possible that it was Grandpa's diary?"

"I am not sure. My mom's last request before she passed away was to bury a small box with her. She said the box held the bad and good memories in her life," Jana said. She poured some tea for Marek and herself.

"Yes, I remember the night before my marriage to your father, she took me to her room. She took the box out, found this ring, and gave it to me. She said the ring was from her mother. It seemed she treated the box like it was precious," Jana continued and showed Marek the ring on her finger.

"What else was in the box, Mom?"

"I don't have any idea. I didn't see inside. When it was buried with my mom, it was already locked and none of us had a key," Jana replied.

"Is it possible there was a diary of Grandpa's in the box?" Marek asked.

"I don't know, Marek. Actually, nobody knows. Why do you ask all of these questions?" Jana replied.

"Mom! Remember I told you that the funeral scene in my dreams is now appearing often during my meditation? Not only that, I have started experiencing another scene during my meditation. These scenes have become clearer and feel more real each time I see them. The most amazing thing is, though, is that while I couldn't monitor what was happening in my dream, I can direct my thinking during my meditation. And I can remember almost everything clearly after meditation. In the past, when I woke up from dreams in my sleep, everything was a blur." Marek sipped some tea from his cup.

"When I've meditated the last few days, I keep looking at my mom, I mean Great-Grandma Klara, at the funeral. Once I look at her, the other scene appears, and I am with Grandma Darina talking about some secret bank code and a diary. It has happened almost every time when I meditate. It seems like some spirit is trying to tell me something important. Remember I told you before that in the dream I am Grandpa Pavel?" Marek continued.

"Are you talking about the secret code for the Swiss bank account? Do you think the secret code was written in the diary? Is that what you think?" Jana asked.

"I believe so and I hope so, Mom," Marek replied.

EXPLORATION

After Marek thought about it for a few days more, he again went to talk to his mom.

"Mom, you know my company is close to bankruptcy. If I don't find the money to save it, it will be the end of my career," he said.

"Yes, I've known that for a while already. I'm very sorry that I can't offer you any help," Jana said.

"I'm thinking of holding a family meeting, including Uncle Franda and Uncle Lomy. I want to propose to them that we dig up Grandma's coffin to see if there is any diary in her box."

"What did you say? Are you crazy?!"

"No, Mom! You know there is a chance that the secret code to the Swiss bank account was written in that diary."

"But we should not disturb the dead! Especially your own family! Your uncles will not approve of your idea. Furthermore, if you tell them about the secret code and diary, they will not believe you anyway. They will think it's your imagination and your problem. Definitely, they will think you are crazy."

"Mom, I have put a lot of thought into this. I've done some research in the last few days, and I know that the cemetery where Grandma was buried is always saturated with water. It's located in a low area. We can just tell my uncles that it is not good for Grandma's soul living in such a damp place, and that we intend to move her to a better place."

"Marek. All right, it's not a problem for me. But you must find your own way to convince your two uncles. Without their approval, you cannot touch Grandma's grave."

PERSUASION

Marek's first uncle, Franda, was already 71 years old and living with his son in the San Francisco area. Franda had two children - a boy, Michael, and a girl, Christine. Both Michael and Christine were married. Michael had two young daughters while Christine did not have any children yet.

Marek's second uncle, Lomy, was 69. He lived in a Chicago suburb. Lomy had two sons, Thomas and Peter. One had just gotten married while the younger one was still single.

Marek decided to convince his younger uncle first since he was in the Chicago area.

"Hey! Uncle Lomy. I haven't seen you in a long time. How are you doing?" Marek called him on the phone.

"Hi, Marek, my favorite nephew. How is your mom? We should see each other more often. You know, when you are getting older, you miss more of your old friends and relatives," Lomy said.

"Great! This is the reason I'm calling you. Mom misses you very much too. She's always told me that you were her favorite. Both of you could talk all day long without feeling tired," Marek said.

"Ha, ha, ha! That's right. We talked about everything, you know. Have ever since we were small."

"Are you available this weekend? I can come to pick you up and drop you off. Mom said you don't like to drive much anymore, especially at nighttime."

"Sure! It will be so great to see her again. You know, it's been nearly eight months since we last saw each other. It seems we live so close in Chicago, yet so far," Lomy replied.

"I'll pick you up at 10 on Sunday morning. Okay?"

"Okay, I'll be ready for you."

"By the way," Marek said, casually introducing the real reason for the upcoming visit, "Mom and I have something to talk to you about. You know Grandma's grave? I investigated last week and discovered that that area is always covered by water, a damp place."

"Isn't the spot where she was buried higher than the surrounding area?"

"Yes. But Mom said the underground water might still cause dampness in Grandma's grave. She feels Grandma's soul should not be around the water. I found a new place that is nice and dry with a good view. Mom and I are thinking about moving Grandma's grave to this new place," Marek went on.

"Let's talk about it when we meet this weekend. If possible, maybe you could show me the new place."

Meeting with Lomy

In order to convince his uncles, Marek had gone to the effort of actually finding a nice cemetery, Irving Park Cemetery, the week before. Though it was a little bit farther away, it was dry and really did have a better view.

Marek went to his uncle's place to pick him up on Sunday morning, May 11, 2003. It was a beautiful, sunny day. He brought his uncle back home where his mom was already there and waiting. As soon as Marek opened the door, Jana stepped forward to give Lomy a hug and welcome him.

"Lomy, my little brother! It is so great to see you," Jana said.

"I'm not little anymore, Jana," Lomy laughed.

"To me, you are always my little brother."

The three of them moved into the living room where Erik and Steffen were watching TV.

Erik immediately pounced on Lomy. "Hi, Great-Uncle! Did you bring us anything this time?" he asked.

"Yes, of course I did," Lomy responded, producing some chocolate from his bag. "I know you like this kind, right?"

"Yes, it's the best kind in the world! You always bring us the best chocolate. But it's so expensive! Thank you, Great-Uncle!" Steffen got up to give his uncle a big hug, and also to get the chocolate.

"Hi, Uncle Lomy, I heard you come in. My, it's nice to see you. I was in the kitchen in the middle of cooking lunch. We should be ready to eat by noon," Stephanie told him.

"Gosh, it smells good! You are a wonderful chef. Nobody can cook as well as you, especially when you are making something Italian. Right? I can smell it!" Lomy said.

"Yes, I'm making your favorite Italian dishes - lasagna and stuffed calamari in tomato sauce. I also made a nice salad to go with. I hope you like it," she said. Stephanie had become an expert at preparing all the wonderful traditional Italian meals under the tutelage of her mom, who was originally from Italy.

Erik and Steffen headed outside to play with the neighbor kids as soon as lunch was over. While Stephanie was washing up in the kitchen, Marek, his uncle, and his mom went to sit in the living room.

"So, Uncle Lomy, I have some photos of the new cemetery to show you. And here's a report on the conditions at the current cemetery. As you can see, it does have a lot of problems with water," Marek said.

"How much does it cost? I mean, if we decide to move my mom's coffin," Lomy asked.

"It will be about $15,000. That means if you and I and Uncle Franda share in the cost, we'll each pay about $5,000 at most. Since I'm the one proposing we do this, I'll take care of making the arrangements. All you and Uncle Franda would need to do is attend the reburial ceremony when everything is ready," Marek explained.

"Fifteen thousand dollars? That sounds affordable. I'm inclined to say yes, but I'd like to see the new cemetery before I make a final decision. Can you take me there?"

"Of course, Uncle Lomy. It takes about an hour to get there. If we leave here by 3, we can spend 30 minutes or so there, and then I can take you home and get you back before 6 when it starts to get dark and traffic is busy with people returning from their weekend," Marek said.

SEE THE NEW CEMETERY

Marek drove his car through the gate into the cemetery and parked. When they stepped out of the car, a caretaker came over to meet them.

"Mr. Müller? I've been waiting for you. I'm glad you called first to make an appointment. Normally I wouldn't be here since it's Sunday," he greeted them.

"Thank you for coming out, Mr. Taylor, I'm sorry to bother you. We won't be here for long. This is my uncle, and this is my mom. They would like to take a look at the lot I intend to purchase," Marek said.

"No problem, if it doesn't take too long," Mr. Taylor said.

They all climbed back into Marek's car and Mr. Taylor directed them along a winding drive and up a hill to a higher part of the cemetery where there were some nice, big pine trees. As they stepped out of the car once again, Mr. Taylor pointed to a spot a short distance from the tallest tree.

"These are the last two lots available. The original owner moved back to Paris last month. If you want it, you had better decide quickly since these are the two best lots in the entire cemetery," Mr. Taylor said.

"We'll make our decision within a week. Once everyone in the family agrees I'll contact the cemetery committee to finalize the purchase. Thank you for reminding me," Marek said.

"Take your time and look around. I'll be in the car waiting for you," Mr. Taylor replied.

From the look on his face, Marek could tell that his uncle liked the place. It was so quiet and felt peaceful there.

"I like it, Marek," Lomy said after about five minutes of taking in the view.

Jana did not join in the conversation. She was just listening. She felt a little bit guilty because she knew that the real motivation behind buying the new grave site was to create an opportunity to search for the diary that was possibly buried with her mom.

"Would you please talk to Uncle Franda about this?" Marek said. "I think it will be more convincing if you talk to him, especially since you have seen the place and can tell him how wonderful it is."

"I'll call him tonight and see what he says," Lomy answered.

They spent another twenty minutes or so just walking about, curiously inspecting the nearby monuments and enjoying the tranquil atmosphere. Then they left the cemetery and took Uncle Lomy home. It was almost 6 p.m. when they got him back, just in time for dinner with his family. After that, Marek took his mom home. He needed to work the next morning.

PERSUADING FRANDA

"Franda! This is Lomy. It's been a long time. When will you and your family come to visit us again?" Lomy asked when he called his brother that night.

"Wow! This is a surprise. How are you doing? Why are you calling me? Is your second son Peter getting married?" Franda responded with a laugh. He was always joking with his younger brother.

"No! Not yet. He's still in love, though, so soon. Very soon, I would guess. I'll let you know for sure," Lomy replied. "Actually, I called you because there is a family matter that we need your agreement on," Lomy continued.

"What's the problem? You sound serious," Franda said.

"Nothing serious. It's just that Jana mentioned Mom's grave is in a damp area. Jana believes Mom's soul will not like it since it is so wet."

"So, you want to relocate Mom's grave, is that what you're saying? Right. Is there any good cemetery around the Chicago area?" Franda asked.

"Actually, Marek has found a cemetery to the west of Chicago with a very nice empty lot. It's a little bit farther out, but it's very nice," Lomy replied.

"That means you saw it already?"

"Yes, Franda, I saw it this afternoon. It's much better than the place where she is now."

"How much will it cost? I hope it's not too expensive. You know, we aren't making any money at our age. I'm retired."

"It will cost each one of us about $5,000 if we share it. Do you want to come and see the lot yourself? It will be great if you do. Then we can have a nice reunion. Now that we are getting older, I miss you more."

"When were you all thinking of relocating Mom? Soon?" Franda asked.

"Yes. Since it's such a good lot, it can be taken anytime soon. Marek said if you approved, it could be next week," Lomy answered.

"I wouldn't be able to come and see the lot before next week. That's just too rushed. Tell you what? I will definitely come for the reburial ceremony. I would like to see the place and participate."

"Great! Then plan to stay for a couple days more so that we can spend some time together and have a nice chat," Lomy said.

Lomy called Marek as soon as he'd hung up the phone.

"Hi, Marek. Your big uncle said, 'go ahead.' Just do a good job."

"I promise I will, Uncle Lomy. I'll contact the cemetery committee tomorrow and pay a deposit," Marek replied.

"When will we relocate the grave?"

"We will probably bring up Grandma's coffin next week on Friday, if it is sunny. Then the reburial ceremony could be the following day. You know they'll need some time to prepare everything for us."

"Once you have confirmed the dates, please call Uncle Franda. He needs to purchase a plane ticket and make arrangements, you know. The sooner he knows the dates, the better," Lomy said.

"I'll take care of it, Uncle Lomy. Thanks for calling him. Bye!"

Digging

Once Marek had paid the deposit and made arrangements with the people who ran the cemetery, he called his Uncle Franda to confirm the relocation of the grave so that his uncle could buy his airplane ticket. Digging at the old cemetery would begin the following Friday morning. The coffin was to stay in the cemetery's storage building for one night and the reburial ceremony was to be held at 10 the next morning.

That Friday, Marek and his mom were at the old cemetery by 9:30 a.m., standing by the grave waiting anxiously. They did not have to wait long before two cemetery workers with a machine came. It took them about an hour to prepare the site and start digging. Once they reached a certain depth, they shut off the machine and continued to dig by hand so that they wouldn't accidentally break into the coffin. Finally, they wrapped the coffin with rope and used the machine to lift it up out of the ground.

Jana's eyes were red. Watching the workers exhume the coffin had brought back a lot of memories she had of her mom. It had been 20 years already since she died.

"Can you replace the old coffin with a new one? The old one doesn't look like it's in very good shape," Marek asked.

"Yes, we can order one to be ready for you tomorrow. You will have to come early, though, when we move the body from the old cemetery to the new one. That's the rule here," one worker said.

"Of course. How early should we come? 8 or 9 a.m.?"

"Eight is better. That will give us more time to prepare," he replied. "Actually, you should let us move this coffin to the new cemetery today. There's a mortuary there," he continued.

"Okay. We'll follow you there. We need to take a look at the inside of the casket when we are there," Marek said. He struggled to hide his anxiety about the box that was buried with his grandma.

"We understand," the other worker said.

The workers put the coffin into a hearse and drove off. Marek and his mom got in their car and followed them out to the new cemetery. The drive took almost an hour. Once they arrived, two other workers were there waiting for them.

The coffin was carefully lifted out of the hearse by the workers from the old cemetery and placed on a carrier that the new cemetery workers had with them. The coffin was then brought into a building and placed in the center of the room. Aside from Jana's Mom's coffin, the room was empty. Since there were almost no sites left available at the cemetery, the room was very rarely used.

"Would you please open it? I would like to take a look," Marek said.

It was not uncommon for people to ask for this when they brought in an exhumed coffin for reburial. Families didn't like leaving the coffins alone with strangers without first inspecting them to see if anything valuable had been buried inside with the body. There could be jewelry or other precious items that might be stolen.

"No problem, Mr. Müller!"

The workers opened the coffin carefully. Marek's heart was beating so fast it felt like it was going to jump out of his throat. He tried to be calm. He knew all his family's secrets could be hidden inside of the box that had been buried with his grandma. Jana just watched the proceedings with tears in her eyes.

Once the coffin was opened, first they saw the skeleton of his grandma's body and then, resting beside it, the box. It had been 20 years under the ground.

"I'll take this box and keep it tonight. I'll bring it back tomorrow for the reburial. My grandma liked to always have this box with her. There are a lot of memories in this box," Marek explained to the workers.

"We understand. We just need you to sign this form and then you can take it with you," a worker said as he retrieved the form from a desk in the corner of the room.

SECRET IN THE BOX

Once he was back at home Marek tried to open the box, but it was locked, and the lock was rusty. He didn't want to force it open since that might damage the box. Instead, he took the box to a locksmith who was able to open it for him easily. The locksmith also made a key for him. Since the locksmith was standing there watching, Marek took just a quick look inside of the box. He saw a handkerchief, some gem-stones, a pile of letters, and many other items. But he didn't immedi-ately see a diary, which worried and disappointed him. He didn't want to turn the box upside down and dump out the contents right there, so he closed it up again and brought it home.

As soon as Marek walked in his front door at home, he found his mom there waiting for him.

"Marek! Have you found the diary inside the box?" Jana asked.

"No, Mom. It's just filled up with various things and a pile of let-ters," Marek replied disappointedly.

"Did you check all the way to the bottom? That diary was so pre-cious to Grandma, she would have put it on the very bottom of the box to hide it," Jana reminded him.

"No, I didn't check the bottom. I didn't want to pull everything out in front of the locksmith at the store."

"Here. Let's take all of the things out and place them on the table carefully. We'll check together," Jana said.

Marek took the items out of the box one by one and arranged them carefully on the table. When he reached the bottom, he smiled up at his mom.

"There are some books here on the bottom, Mom," Marek said ex-citedly.

He took out two books and opened one carefully. The books were the diaries they were looking for! One was completely filled with writ-ing, while the other was only half full.

"I'll take these two diaries to a professional copy shop to get them copied and scanned. I'll also take a photo of each page. You know, Mom, just to be cautious. These diaries could be very important to us," Marek said. He carefully put the two books in a plastic bag that he then tucked into his business briefcase.

He spent the whole afternoon at a copy shop, vigilantly monitoring the worker there who copied and scanned the diaries. If the worker wasn't very careful, the books could be damaged. After all, they had been underground for a long period of time.

As he watched the copying process, Marek could see a lot of writing that wasn't recognizable to him. To start with, the ink was fading out and the writings were blurred. In addition to that, the writing was in the Western Slavik language, which he couldn't read.

Once he was back home, Marek took a photo of each page as a final precaution; this was just too important to him. When he was finished with that, he carefully put the diaries back into the bottom of his grandma's box and arranged the other items on the top. Then he re-locked the box using the key the locksmith had provided him.

Now he needed to spend some time trying to find the possible secret hidden in these two diaries. He would need his mom to translate the contents for him. Jana was 26 years old when her family had immigrated to the U.S. in 1954. She could read Western Slavik very well.

That evening Marek went to O'Hare International Airport to pick up his Uncle Franda, whose plane was arriving at 9:30 p.m. Franda had come alone; since this was a reburial, his two children and their families had stayed behind. Marek brought him to stay at his sister's home with his mom, Jana. They would have a great gathering.

REBURIAL

Saturday morning, May 24, 2003, Marek, his wife and two sons went to Irving Park Cemetery at 8 a.m., bringing with them the box. His sister, Susan, would be arriving with his mom and Uncle Franda around 9:30 a.m. Naturally his second uncle, Lomy, and Lomy's younger son, Peter, would also be there.

When Marek arrived, the same two workers from the day before were there with a new coffin. As Marek watched, they gently removed the delicate skeleton from the old coffin and transferred it to the new. Marek then placed the box back in his grandma's coffin. The workers sealed the coffin, then put it in the hearse to drive to the burial site.

At the site, a new grave had been dug the day before and everything was ready. A preacher had been hired to say a few words for this ceremony, and Marek had arranged for many baskets with a variety of flowers to decorate the site. By 10 a.m., everyone was there. They greeted each other solemnly, then turned their attention to the preacher. By 10:45, the ceremony was over

CHAPTER 8. SECRET CODE

During this time, Marek's business had continued to deteriorate without any sign of recovery. According to the news on TV many companies, including some big ones, had had to file Chapter 11 bankruptcy. Marek's worry grew. Due to that, and to a lack of rest, he kept losing weight. His health declined. He had developed a gastric ulcer nearly a year ago. It seemed that he had aged so much in just two years. Naturally, Jana was worried about her son as well. The only moments of peace Marek could find were during his early meditation time each day.

But now Marek had his grandpa's diaries. The thought of them made him both excited and anxious. He had put all of his hopes into these diaries, but because of his limited understanding of the Western Slavik language, he couldn't read them. He needed his mom to translate them for him. From his meditation and analysis, he knew that the most important dates on which to look for information would be around his grandma's birthday in 1928, the year his grandpa opened the Swiss bank account.

On Monday morning, instead of going to work, Marek planned to bring a copy of the diaries to his mom. Although he was excited to delve into them, he also worried about whether or not he would be able to find the secret code. Before he went to see her, he called her.

"Mom! I can't read most of Grandpa's diaries. They are written in the Western Slavik language. I need you to translate them for me. Can I come to see you this morning?"

"Don't you have to work, Marek? It's Monday."

"Mom! I think this is more important than my business right now. If there is any hope to save my company, it will be in these diaries."

"Okay! I'll be waiting for you."

Immediately Marek left and went to see his mom. When he arrived, Jana was waiting for him. His sister Susan was at school teaching, so there was no one else around.

"Mom, can we sit at the dining table? I need to type down every word you translate into my laptop computer. This is very important."

"Where should we start? There's so much written in the diary."

"Let's begin in the year 1928 when Grandpa opened the Swiss bank account."

Jana nodded her head and opened one of the copied diaries. This was the older one and all the pages were full of words. Jana found the pages where the year 1928 started and began to translate them word for word, which Marek then immediately entered into his computer.

Jana read for quite a while without any mention of a Swiss bank secret code. Marek was a little bit disappointed. Jana had translated every page until they were near the end of the year, October 30, 1928. Still nothing was found.

"Mom, when was Grandma's birthday? That's probably the most important date that we should look for."

"She was born on November 20, 1896."

"Okay, Mom! Let's go to that page, and please be careful now to translate every word clearly."

Jana went to the designated spot and continued to read but at a much slower speed so that Marek would not miss a single word. However, when Jana began to read what was written on the 20th of November, "Today is Darina's 31st birthday. We had a small party at home..."

"Stop! Mom! Did you say Grandma's birthday was November 20th of 1896?" Marek abruptly interrupted.

"Yes, Marek. What's wrong?"

"Mom, then Grandma should be 32 years old instead of 31. Right?"

"Oh! Yes. I wasn't paying attention to that, Marek." Jana nodded her head and paused for a moment. "That's strange! As I know from my mom, your grandpa was very careful and precise about everything. He wouldn't make a mistake like this. It's too obvious, especially to get his wife's age wrong," Jana said.

"Can you read the next page and see if there are any other mistakes that are obvious?" Marek asked.

"Let me take a look," Jana said and read through the diary of the following day. After a couple minutes she went on, "Here is another mistake. He mentions his father's accident happening when he was 37 years old. But I know that he was 33 years old when it happened."

"Mom, I think these are clues. He wrote in these mistakes on purpose. Only those who knew the truth of the family's history would recognize these mistakes. If I'm correct, the first two number of the code may be 1 and 7. Mom, please read the next day's entry," Marek said excitedly.

"Yes! There is another mistake on the next page! As I know, this number should be a 7 instead of a 9. I'll keep going. Just write down what I say, Marek."

In some pages, the spellings of names or places were misspelled. This implied some of the code's digits were not numbers but letters.

After 30 minutes, all of the mistakes put together read: 179235P28942W13045T0.

Jana kept going and, page by page, a few more letters were identified. "Here is a U. Then, there is B and next S, then A and G," Jana said.

"Mom, that means 179235P28942W13045T0UBSAG," Marek said.

"There are no more mistakes after that. It's obvious to me, but it wouldn't be to outside people," Jana said.

"Mom, Thank you for your help! I believe that the first 20 digits are the actual code and last few letters may be the bank's name. I will check it out to see if there is a bank or financial company called UBS AG," Marek said.

Using his laptop, he searched the banks listed as being in Switzerland. Eventually he found a Swiss global financial services company called UBS AG. He was so excited.

"Mom, I think I've found it! Here is a financial services company called UBS AG. I'll travel to Geneva next week and see if what we've discovered in the diary is the correct code." Marek was thrilled. He knew that if he was able to withdraw money from his grandpa's account, he could save his company from bankruptcy.

Swiss Bank

On the morning of June 1, 2003, after nearly 13 hours of traveling, Marek arrived in Geneva. He was exhausted when he checked into a hotel, and he really needed a rest, so he took a shower and lay down on the bed. He was very tired but, at the same time, so excited to be there that he could not sleep well. In fact, he hadn't slept well for over a week. June 1 was a Sunday and all of the banks were closed so that there was nothing he could do but wait until the next day and try to relax in the meantime.

As Marek lay on the bed, he refocused his mind on his deep breathing technique. He inhaled to lead the Qi to his abdominal area and exhaled to lead the Qi to his feet. He knew from his Qigong study that this way would help him calm his mind. Although this way hadn't worked for him all last week, now he tried again and only paid attention to his deep breathing and, at the same time, to leading the Qi downward. Gradually he fell asleep.

When he woke up it was around 2 in the morning. His mind was clear, and he knew he would not fall asleep again, but he had had a nice, sound sleep for eight hours. The idea of going to the bank in the morning filled him with anticipation, though he was not 100% sure whether or not the code was correct.

"Will they reject my request to access the account? Will the code be correct? After all, the account was opened 75 years ago." The more Marek thought of it, the more worry shaded his excitement. He had made an appointment with one of the bank managers, Mr. Schmit, last Friday on the phone.

"I hope everything goes smoothly," he thought.

A SURPRISE

By 9:50 that morning he was standing in front of the door of the building where UBS AG Financial Services had their offices. Just inside the door he found a service desk with a lady seated behind it.

"Hi! I have an appointment with Mr. Schmit at 10 a.m.," Marek said to the lady.

"I'll let him know you're here. Can I have your name, sir?" she asked.

"Marek, Marek Müller, ma'am," he replied.

She placed a call, then turned back to Marek. "Mr. Schmit will be here in a couple of minutes," she said.

Five minutes later, a middle-aged gentleman appeared in the hall.

"You must be Mr. Müller. I am Mr. Schmit, the assistant manager of this financial service company. Would you please come with me to my office?" the gentleman said and led Marek down the hall to his office.

"Now, what can I do for you, Mr. Müller?" Mr. Schmit asked once they were seated.

"My grandpa opened an account here a long time ago. I would like to try and see if I am able to access it," Marek said.

"Do you have the bank code?" Mr. Schmit asked.

"Yes, at least, I hope this is the code," Marek said as he handed Mr. Schmit a piece of paper with the secret code written on it.

Mr. Schmit glanced at what was written on the paper, then looked back up at Marek in surprise.

"This is a very old bank account code. Do you know when your grandfather opened his account with us?" Mr. Schmit asked.

"It would have been in 1928, 75 years ago," Marek replied.

"I'll have to do some investigating. Please wait for a few minutes. I'll be right back," Mr. Schmit said.

It appeared as though Mr. Schmit had some reservations about Marek's grandpa's account since there had not been any activity on it for nearly 50 years. While Marek waited anxiously, Mr. Schmit left to check their records and to confer with the manager.

When he returned, he said, "Mr. Müller, as you know, we only honor and recognize the secret bank code at that time. Your code does indeed match an account that was opened in 1928. For verification, what was your grandfather's name, Mr. Müller?" Mr. Schmit asked.

"His name was Pavel Damet, Mr. Schmit," Marek replied.

"Well! It looks like everything is correct. Do you know how much money is in this account?"

"I have no idea, Mr. Schmit. My grandpa died suddenly of a heart attack while he was in Paris in 1952." Marek's own heart leapt to his throat in his excitement.

"Your grandfather's account has about $640 million in the bank. What do you want to do with it, Mr. Müller?" Mr. Schmit asked.

"I need to talk to my uncles and my mom. They have a right to this money as well and should know about this. But, would it be possible for me to take $10,000 out of the account today?" Marek asked.

"Of course, I can get that ready for you. I will need your passport, fingerprints, and also a drop of blood for DNA. You know, for future identity recognition. If you will wait here one more time, I will ask a company nurse to come and collect a drop of blood from your finger tip," Mr. Schmit said and left once again.

A few minutes later a nurse came in and introduced herself.

"Hello, Mr. Müller, my name is Laura. I'm just going to swab your fingertip, then you will feel a little pinch," she said.

"No, problem. I'm ready."

Laura wiped Marek's second finger with an antibacterial swab, then used a needle to prick it and collect a drop of blood. "That's all done. Mr. Schmit will be right back," she said and left.

Mr. Schmit soon returned with an ink pad and some paperwork, which he handed to Marek.

"Please fill out this form, and then we will take a print of your right index finger," Mr. Schmit said.

After Marek had finished, Mr. Schmit double-checked the information on the form against the information on Marek's passport. He needed to be sure that there were no mistakes.

"Here is a bank draft for $10,000 as you requested. I'll be waiting for your further contact about what to do with the rest of the money. Also, here is my business card. You may call me directly or e-mail me," Mr. Schmit said.

"Thank you very much, sir," Marek said. "I appreciate your help."

Marek had never felt so great in the last two years. He knew that everything would be fine from now on. As he walked out of the building, he couldn't stop smiling. It had been a long, long time since he had last felt like this - so worry-free and light, just like a bird.

Marek was on the very next flight back to Chicago. He didn't call his mom while he was in Geneva. It would take too long to explain and, besides, he felt it wouldn't be secure speaking about it over the phone.

CHAPTER 9. HAPPY ENDING

As soon as he got home, Marek called his first uncle in San Francisco. "Uncle Franda, will you have time to come to Chicago for an emergency family meeting?"

"What's the problem this time? Is it about Grandma's new grave? We just reburied her a couple weeks ago," Franda asked with curiosity.

"No, Uncle Franda, it's not about the grave. It's about Grandpa's fortune. I can't explain it clearly over the phone. Plus, it's too risky talking about it on the phone," Marek said.

"All right. How about next Sunday, June 8th? Once I get my ticket, I'll call you to let you know what time my flight arrives. I'll need you to pick me up at O'Hare airport."

"Okay. I'll wait to hear from you. I'm going to contact Uncle Lomy as well. I know that you, Uncle Lomy, and mom must be together to make decisions about something this big."

"Uncle Lomy! This is Marek. Would you be able to come to my house for another family meeting next Sunday morning, June 8th? Uncle Franda will fly back to Chicago as well."

"What's the occasion this time? Your mom's birthday? Your sister finally is going to get married, right?" Uncle Lomy joked with Marek.

"No, Uncle Lomy! This is not something to joke about. We need to meet to talk about Grandpa's fortune in the Swiss bank," Marek said.

"Why? I thought we lost all that money since we didn't have the secret bank code," Lomy said.

"We'll talk about it in more detail when we meet. Okay?"

"Okay. I'll be there. This is a surprise, the second reunion of the family in three weeks," Lomy said.

HAPPY ENDING

Marek went to O'Hare airport to pick up his uncle at 7:30 p.m. on Saturday, June 7, 2003 and brought him back to his home. Marek's mom was waiting there. Naturally, Marek had already told her everything as soon as he returned from Geneva. Jana was very excited. At least, she was very happy that the money her father had worked so hard to earn had not been lost. But more importantly for her was seeing her son's smile return now that his company had been saved.

The next morning, Lomy was dropped off at Marek's house by his son, Peter. After their arrival Marek took his uncles and mom to his study to talk. It would be easier to have a private conversation there than in the living room, where Marek's kids were playing.

"Uncles, first I want to apologize for misleading you about the main reason for relocating Grandma's grave. The reason we gave you, that the original place was too damp, was true. But in addition, I was hoping to find some clue about the secret code to Grandpa's Swiss bank from Grandpa's diary. We didn't tell you this from the beginning because, well, first, Mom and I weren't sure if the diary was even there inside the box that was buried with Grandma. Second, even if we had the diary, we weren't sure if we could find the secret code from it. And third, we were afraid that you wouldn't allow us to open the coffin if you knew our intention. I'm very sorry, Uncles." Marek took a break and glanced at his uncles' facial expressions. They looked disappointed, and a little bit upset. But even as he watched, their expressions changed into looks full of curiosity.

"Actually, Mom and I did find the diaries in the box, just as we hoped. They were written in Western Slavik, which Mom helped me to translate. At first, we found nothing that even suggested a bank code. But eventually I found a clue to how the code was written in. The bank secret code, along with the name of the bank UBS AG, was hidden within 20 different days of diary entries. After I found it, I went to Geneva and talked to the UBS AG manager. I was so surprised when he told me that the code was accurate. He also told me Grandpa had about $640 million in the bank. While I was there, I withdrew $10,000 just to prove that I was able to access this account. Here's the bank draft for the withdrawal, Uncles." Marek did not tell them that how he had actually found the code - how he even knew to look for the code - was through his meditation practice and the dreams of his grandpa he had had while sleeping. They might laugh at him. He would wait to tell them some other time, if they asked.

Both Marek's uncles were shocked by the news. All they had ever known was that their father had saved a lot of money in a Swiss bank. But they also knew that the secret code to the bank account had been lost due to their father's sudden death. Lomy and Franda sat quite still for a while and looked at each other. They knew all of that money now belonged to the three surviving children.

"This is a very big surprise, Marek," Franda finally said.

"The question now is, how do you want to divide the money and what will you do with it? Once you have decided that, you know, we will need to go to Geneva to straighten it out with the UBS AG financial service company," Marek explained.

"I suggest that we divide it into four parts. One part should belong to Marek. You know, without him, this money would never have returned to us." Lomy looked at Franda and Jana. Naturally, Jana agreed since Marek needed this money for his company. In addition, it was the truth that without Marek, this money would never have been recovered.

"I agree it's only fair that Marek receives a share," Franda said with a smile.

"That means each one of us should have $160 million. That's a lot of money. I think I am going to have a heart attack," Lomy laughed.

CONCLUSION

On Sunday, June 15, 2003, all four of them flew first class to Geneva. Now they could afford a little bit of luxury. The next day, on Monday morning, they went to the bank to see Mr. Schmit. Marek had called him the previous week to make an appointment.

As he had done on Marek's previous visit, Mr. Schmit checked all of their passports, and collected their fingerprints and some blood for DNA. Then they were given a secret code for each of their new accounts. They would be able to withdraw money anytime they wanted directly through internet access.

As Marek, Jana, Franda and Lomy stepped out of the bank, they felt the sun shining on their faces. Now Marek truly understood that what he had encountered for his business problem had been caused by the energy imbalance of his grandpa's sudden death. Now his grandpa's fortune was reclaimed, and the new balance was regained. Marek also knew what he wanted when he retired: he would move to the mountain and continue his search for his spiritual understanding.

ABOUT THE AUTHOR

Dr. Yang, Jwing-Ming was born on August 11, 1946, in Xinzhu Xian (新竹縣), Taiwan (台灣), Republic of China (中華民國). He started his wushu (武術) (gongfu or kung fu, 功夫) training at the age of fifteen under Shaolin White Crane (Shaolin Bai He, 少林白鶴) Master Cheng, Gin-Gsao (曾金灶). Master Cheng originally learned taizuquan (太祖拳) from his grandfather when he was a child. When Master Cheng was fifteen years old, he started learning White Crane from Master Jin, Shao-Feng (金紹峰) and followed him for twenty-three years until Master Jin's death.

In thirteen years of study (1961–1974) under Master Cheng, Dr. Yang became an expert in the White Crane style of Chinese martial arts, which includes both the use of bare hands and various weapons, such as saber, staff, spear, trident, two short rods, and many others. With the same master, he also studied White Crane qigong (白鶴氣功), qin na or chin na (擒拿), tui na (推拿), and dian xue massages (點穴按 摩) and herbal treatment.

At sixteen, Dr. Yang began the study of Yang-style taijiquan (楊氏 太極拳) under Master Kao Tao (高濤). He later continued his study of taijiquan under Master Li, Mao- Ching (李茂清). Master Li learned his taijiquan from the well-known Master Han, Ching-Tang (韓慶堂). From this further practice, Dr. Yang was able to master the taiji bare-hand sequence, pushing hands, the two-man fighting sequence, taiji sword, taiji saber, and taiji qigong.

When Dr. Yang was eighteen years old, he entered Tamkang College (淡江學院) in Taipei Xian to study physics. In college, he began the study of traditional Shaolin Long Fist (Changquan or Chang Chuan, 長拳) with Master Li, Mao-Ching at the Tamkang College Guoshu Club (淡江國術社), 1964–1968, and eventually became an assistant instructor under Master Li. In 1971 he completed his MS degree in physics at the National Taiwan University (台灣大學) and then served in the Chinese Air Force from 1971 to 1972. In the service, Dr. Yang taught physics at the Junior Academy of the Chinese Air Force (空軍幼校) while also teaching wushu. After being honorably discharged in 1972, he returned to Tamkang College to teach physics and resumed study under Master Li, Mao-Ching. From Master Li, Dr. Yang learned Northern-style Wushu, which includes bare-hand and kicking techniques as well as numerous weapons.

In 1974 Dr. Yang came to the United States to study mechanical engineering at Purdue University. At the request of a few students, Dr. Yang began to teach gongfu (kung fu), which resulted in the establishment of the Purdue University Chinese Kung Fu Research Club in the spring of 1975. While at Purdue, Dr. Yang also taught college-credit courses in taijiquan. In May 1978, he was awarded a PhD in mechanical engineering by Purdue.

In 1980 Dr. Yang moved to Houston to work for Texas Instruments. While in Houston, he founded Yang's Shaolin Kung Fu Academy, which was eventually taken over by his disciple, Mr. Jeffery Bolt, after Dr. Yang moved to Boston in 1982. Dr. Yang founded Yang's Martial Arts Academy in Boston on October 1, 1982.

In January 1984, he gave up his engineering career to devote more time to research, writing, and teaching. In March 1986, he purchased property in the Jamaica Plain area of Boston to be used as the headquarters of the new organization, Yang's Martial Arts Association (YMAA). The organization expanded to become a division of Yang's Oriental Arts Association, Inc. (YOAA).

In 2008 Dr. Yang began the nonprofit YMAA California Retreat Center. This training facility in rural California is where selected students enroll in a five-year to ten-year residency to learn Chinese martial arts.

Dr. Yang has been involved in traditional Chinese wushu since 1961, studying Shaolin White Crane (Bai He), Shaolin Long Fist (Changquan), and taijiquan under several different masters. He has taught for more than forty-six years: seven years in Taiwan, five years at Purdue University, two years in Houston, twenty-six years in Boston, and more than eight years at the YMAA California Retreat Center. He has taught seminars all over the world, sharing his knowledge of Chinese martial arts and qigong in Argentina, Austria, Barbados, Botswana, Belgium, Bermuda, Brazil, Canada, China, Chile, England, Egypt, France, Germany, Hungary, Iceland, Ireland, Italy, Latvia, Mexico, the Netherlands, New Zealand, Poland, Portugal, Saudi Arabia, South Africa, Spain, Switzerland, and Venezuela.

Since 1986 YMAA has become an international organization, which currently includes more than fifty schools located in Argentina, Belgium, Canada, Chile, France, Hungary, Iran, Ireland, Italy, New Zealand, Poland, Portugal, South Africa, Sweden, the United Kingdom, the United States, and Venezuela.

Many of Dr. Yang's books and videos have been translated into other languages, such as French, Italian, Spanish, Polish, Czech, Bulgarian, Russian, German, and Hungarian.

For more books by Dr. Yang, Jwing-Ming please go to the YMAA Publishing website. https://ymaa.com/publishing